Death by Cutting Table

by

Susie Black

Holly Swimsuit Mystery, Book Four

Death by Cutting Table

Cover Art by *The Wild Rose Press, Inc.*

The Wild Rose Press, Inc.
PO Box 708
Adams Basin, NY 14410-0708
Visit us at www.thewildrosepress.com

Publishing History
First Edition, 2023
Trade Paperback ISBN 978-1-5092-4845-2
Digital ISBN 978-1-5092-4846-9

Holly Swimsuit Mystery, Book Four
Published in the United States of America

The fireman pointed to the marine power cable connected from the outlet to my boat. The interior guts of the marine cable were covered by a protective rubber encasement. The cable was slit open, exposing the wiring inside mid-cable to the prongs of the tampered plug. Several strips of aluminum foil anchored in place by a fistful of pennies laid on the dock adjacent to the breaker box.

The fireman said, "Whoever did this is no amateur. They knew exactly what they were doing. If they hadn't been interrupted, they would've jammed the pennies in the breakers and wrapped the breakers with the aluminum foil. The breaker would've blown and ignited a fire. With the rubber-coated power cable serving as a connector, the fiberglass boat would've burned to a crisp in a matter of minutes." He stroked his gloved hand across Siggie's head. "It's a darned good thing Ms. Schlivnik's dog scared them off." He turned one-eighty around the basin. "With all the gasoline-powered motors, they came within a hair of blowing up the dock and burning this entire basin to ashes." The fireman shoved his helmet to the crown of his head and whistled through a gap in his front teeth. "Somebody wanted Ms. Schlivnik dead. They came mighty close to succeeding."

Praise for Susie Black

"She may be short of stature, but Holly Schlivnik has attitude to spare."
~ *Ellen Byerrum, author Crime of Fashion series*

"The well-drawn suspects kept me guessing throughout the story."
~ *Nancy J. Cohen, author of the Bad Hair Day Mysteries*

"Who knew the swimsuit business was so full of intrigue?"
~ *Charlotte Rains Dixon, author Emma Jean's Bad Behavior*

"Holly Schlivnik always gets the bad guy before the detective does."
~*Kim Hunt Harris, author The Trailer Park Princess Mysteries*

"Susie Black belongs in your Kindle today!"
~*Elise Sax, author Matchmaker Mystery Series*

"A colorful cast of well-hewn characters makes for a great twisty, turny tale of murder."
~*Nellie H. Steele, author The Cate Kensie Mysteries*

Dedication

This book is dedicated to the devoted staff of the Sirena Apparel Group whose unwavering loyalty, unbreakable moral compass, courageous grace under fire, and tireless efforts to go above and beyond the call of duty reset the bar for those who follow to strive for.

Chapter One

Maybe those big honkin' cutting shears plunged deep into his chest were the first clue. It was pretty obvious there was no big rush to check his pulse. You wouldn't need an MD written after your name to see that Mermaid Swimwear CEO Butch Oldham was as dead as it gets. With a head too big for his short, squatty body, bearded Butch Oldham was, pardon the pun, a dead ringer for a hairier Humpty Dumpty gone to seed.

He lay picture-framed by a large swath of blood-stained swimwear fabrics. His body lay splayed out on the fabric cutting table like one of the mounted butterflies in his office display. His extremities were held in place by four sets of eye pins, one set per extremity. His hands were pinned down at the palms. His bare feet were turned out and secured to the table by eye pins with ribbons of fabric threads wrapped around them pushed through his arches. His pants were pulled down around his ankles, revealing a pair of rather sexy silk black lace-trimmed ladies' panties. His flaccid privates lay squished down outside the right leg opening by the elastic band binding the leg eye.

Naturally, I burst out laughing.

In my defense, let me just say that genetics aren't all they're cracked up to be. Lucky me. I inherited my nana's fear of death we overcompensated for with the nervous habit of laughing.

Before going any further, let me introduce myself and explain the role I play in this tale. I am Holly Schlivnik, President of the private label division of Mermaid Swimwear.

Butch's bluish lips formed an O, as though he was caught by surprise at his situation. With his level of arrogance, no doubt Butch Oldham was quite stunned that someone mustered the nerve to kill him. The rest of us were only stunned it had taken so long.

My boss David Workman, Mermaid Swimwear Corporate President, brought his mentor Benjamin "Butch" Oldham to the company so Butch could protect David from the scrutiny of the board of directors. Too bad for David and the rest of us, Butch had other plans. Butch hoodwinked the board of directors into letting him poach David's position as CEO and took over control of the company. And once he wrapped his tentacles around it, Butch Oldham wasted no time driving the iconic brand and fashion leader of the swimwear industry for almost four decades into the ground while stealing it blindly.

Earlier that fateful afternoon, my colleague Queenie Levine, Mermaid missy division President, went to the fabric storage area of the warehouse to gather prints for a special project. As Queenie later explained, she laid the fabric roll on the cutting table to cut swatches and discovered Butch's splayed-out body nailed to the table. Queenie called my extension and screamed like a crazy woman to come to the warehouse. She dropped the receiver before she said why, but I didn't need any explanations. My pal was in some sort of trouble, and that's all I needed to know. I took off for the warehouse as if my pants had caught on fire. On the way, I ran into Kelly, Butch's trophy wife, wandering around the executive offices looking for her husband. I told Kelly I'd seen Butch headed to the warehouse a few hours ago. I said I was going there and suggested she come along.

I opened the warehouse door leading to the fabric area and shivered as I stuck my head in and looked around. Was it the normal damp coldness of the huge warehouse, or something more sinister sending the involuntary shiver the length of my spine?

I rotated my head periscope-style and formed a megaphone with my hands. "Queenie, where are you?" I shouted at the top of my lungs so she could hear me over the din of the fans swirling twenty-four-seven to keep the inventory from mildewing. She answered in a modulated, robotic-like floating voice similar to one of those electronic disguises kidnappers use to camouflage their identity on the phone. "I'm. Back. Here…"

Tall, statuesque Kelly's long legs took her through the door ahead of me. Halfway between the warehouse door and the fabric-cutting area, Butch's bride screamed and collapsed onto the loose fabric rolls scattered on the warehouse floor. I ran past Kelly and found Queenie standing in front of the cutting table staring at Butch Oldham's corpse.

Her arms were wrapped around her chest and she shivered uncontrollably. There wasn't an ounce of fat on rail-thin Queenie's athletic frame. With no insolation for protection, winter or summer, Queenie is always cold. She kept a sweater in her office and wore it most of the time. The sweater held a special meaning. She graduated with honors from fashion school and the one-of-a-kind sweater she designed won a top award. The drafty warehouse is always cold, so it took me by surprise that Queenie wasn't wearing her sweater. I draped my arm around her shoulders. "You know it's always cold in the warehouse. Why aren't you wearing your sweater? Do you want me to get it for you?"

She whispered, "I've no idea where it is. I went into my office to get it before I came to the warehouse, but I couldn't find it anyplace." This is a first. The sweater is practically her second skin. At some point, she wore it every day.

I dipped my head. "Maybe you took it home to launder?"

She tsked. "No, I laundered it two days ago. I brought it back yesterday."

I shrugged. "It didn't sprout wings. You were in a hurry to get to the warehouse. I'll bet you find it once you search your office more thoroughly."

She said, "I hang it on a hook behind my office door. I never put it anyplace else." Her eyes filled. "I'll die if I can't find it. It's irreplaceable."

I asked, "Do you want me to go look for it now?"

She shook her head and pointed at Butch. "Don't leave me alone with…him."

I squeezed her shoulder and smiled. "Ok. I'm not going anyplace. Don't worry. I'm sure the sweater is someplace in your office. Maybe you were distracted and shoved it in a drawer by accident. I'll help you look for it after we're finished with…" I pointed to the ladies' underwear on the corpse. "Gee, he always seemed to be the boxers kind of guy." Queenie rewarded me with a wan smile and shivered more. So much for levity? Nah. I am a sales exec. Persistence is my middle name. I pointed to the frilly lady's underwear stretched tightly over Butch's privates. "Who knew deep down he turned out to be a lacy panty guy?"

I tossed out my best material, but still got no reaction. Tough audience or something more? Maybe Queenie's shivering had nothing to do with her being cold. With their checkered history, it was common knowledge that there was no love lost between Queenie and Butch. Had Queenie made good on her threat to make Butch pay for destroying our company? I gave her the once-over and breathed a sigh of relief. Her hands were clean, and her clothes weren't covered in Butch's blood. Thank God.

Kelly and Butch were headed for divorce court. On the way to the warehouse, Kelly said she came to the factory to finalize her settlement with Butch. Decades separated them in age. He was a few years past middle age and she was only a few years past drinking age.

Had the much younger and fitter Kelly killed her going-to-seed husband and made up the story of not finding him? Maybe she caught up with him and Butch reneged on their deal. They argued, and she grabbed the cutting shears and killed him in a fit of rage. She changed out of the bloody clothes, stashed them someplace, and went back to the lobby to establish an alibi. Pretty iffy, but they say the spouse is always the prime suspect. Maybe she put on an award-winning performance for my benefit?

Sporting skin-tight animal print leggings and a solid ruffled crop top leaving little to the imagination, Kelly untangled herself from the fabric rolls. She tottered to the cutting table on sexy black sky-high stilettos practically screaming *take me right now*. I stopped her as she reached out for Butch. It was impossible to tell if grief reddened her tear-filled eyes or remorse for murdering her husband?

I'd seen enough *Law & Order* TV episodes to remember not to touch anything and call the cops. With her rubbery arms and legs, Kelly resembled a macabre marionette as she whispered without moving her lips. "I don't feel so good." Kelly's hand shook as she pointed to the warehouse door and whined as cranky as a toddler who needed a nap. "I wanna go home." No kidding, Kel. Get in the boat and row.

I smoothed back a lock of Kelly's bleach-bottle-blonde hair out her swollen azure eyes. "Kelly, I realize this is beyond awful, but we have to wait for the cops."

****

I no sooner dialed nine-one-one and ten minutes later, a squadron of LAPD uniforms arrived. A fire engine, and EMT all with their bubble lights blazing and sirens wailing followed close behind. The band of first responders rushed into the warehouse and found Queenie, Kelly, and me standing transfixed, staring at Butch nailed to the cutting table. I stifled a giggle as the EMT checked Butch's pulse before confirming him deceased to the cops. He must be kidding. Even Hellen Keller could tell Butch Oldham was dead as the proverbial door nail.

Two sets of cops with their guns drawn scoured the building and cleared it. No one told us to reach for the sky, but a uniformed version of Starsky and Hutch demanded to know who we were. As I identified myself, my eyes had a mind of their own. One glance at Butch and off I went to the races. The cops must have wondered whether I was just guilty as sin or just plain crazy. Thank goodness the Assistant Medical Examiner accompanying a gigantic black plainclothes detective happened to be my life-long friend, Sophie Cutler, MD.

I crossed my arms and waved as though guiding an airplane in for a landing and called out, "Hiya Snip."

Tall and powerfully built like a freight train disguised as a linebacker, Detective Josiah Jones allowed the hint of a smile to quirk the corners of his lips as Sophie returned my greeting. He turned to my favorite doc and jerked his chin my way. "Snip? Sophie, you know her? She's the one who called it in."

Sophie rolled her eyes. "Oh, yeah. Do I ever. We met as lab partners in Mr. Hepburn's eighth grade biology class. The thought of cutting up a frog made her squeamish and I couldn't write a proper essay to save my life. We made quite a scholastic tag team. She wrote my essays and I dissected her frog." Sophie shrugged. "That's why I got tagged with the nickname snip."

Detective Jones pinned me with a look saying, "don't move." As if. Then he and Sophie walked over to Butch. Jones leaned over the spread-eagled corpse speared to the table and whistled through a wide space between his front teeth. The detective shook his bald, bowling ball-sized head and muttered. "Only in LA." Jones cocked a brow at Sophie and smirked. "Guess a cause of death is no mystery. What about a time of death?"

Sophie bent over Butch. "This one's pretty fresh. Two hours, maybe less."

Graceful for a big man, Jones swiveled his massive body in my direction and pierced me with an incredulous stare. My dear pal no doubt explained my laughing affliction. Good grief. The cop was grinning from ear to ear. Must she tell the way I laughed myself silly at her Grandma Esther's funeral? Crap, now the cop became flat-out hysterical. Fanfreakingfabulous. She got, no doubt, to the part when her uncle almost threw me out of the chapel. Friends. Go figure.

Once she'd completed my humiliation, Sophie focused her attention back on the corpse and Jones headed my way. Jones angled his big head over at Sophie and smiled a toothy smile. "Really? Snip?"

I grinned and lifted a shoulder. "If the scalpel fits…"

Jones took a small notebook out of his jacket and uncapped a pen with his teeth. "Who's in charge?" The detective rolled his eyes as I pointed to Butch. "Funny. Not. Let me clarify the question. Is anyone who's *vertical* in charge and around?"

Jones pinched his forehead into a frown when I shook my head no. He dipped his head to Butch. "Who is he?"

"Butch Oldham. He's our CEO."

Jones asked. "So, who's in charge now?"

"Mr. Smythe actually runs the company."

Jones blinked his confusion.

I explained the company's situation. "The company is in bankruptcy. Mr. Smythe is the court-appointed administrator." I checked my watch. It was way past office hours. "I've no idea how to reach Mr. Smythe, but I can get my boss David Workman on the phone."

****

I took a double-take as David followed Mr. Smythe into the warehouse. The normally impeccable David Workman's head of wavy salt and pepper hair stood on end as though he'd stuck his finger in a light socket. Mr. Smythe was no different than usual. Nothing shook his foundations. The slightly built, nerdy, circumspect administrator casually glanced over his wireframe glasses at Butch and calmly offered Jones his right hand.

After Jones spoke with David and Mr. Smythe, the detective turned his attention back to Queenie, Kelly, and me. Jones had kept us separated and interviewed Queenie first, since she'd found the body. He finished with Queenie, then Jones requestioned me. Since I'd come into the scene at the end of the movie, I wasn't able to answer most of Jones' additional questions. The detective closed his notepad and dismissed me for the time being, but asked me to stick around in case more questions arose. I wouldn't be getting home anytime soon, so I called my dock neighbor Muriel Lobowsky and asked her to feed and walk my standard poodle/psychiatrist Sigmund.

Jones walked Butch's bride to the corner desk and asked Kelly, "You're the victim's wife? I'm sorry for your loss." Jones smiled at Kelly when she numbly nodded yes, but the smile never made it to his eyes. "I'll try to keep this as short as possible." An hour later, a ghost-white Mrs. Oldham shook like a leaf in a thunderstorm when Jones dismissed her with the admonishment not to leave town.

The crime scene team photographed Butch, the cutting table, and the warehouse. Then one of them drew those chalk marks around Butch the way you see them do on TV. The lead CSI took Butch's fingerprints and then tied plastic bags over Butch's hands. The guy nodded to Sophie and she gave the ok to move Butch. A CSI assistant brought in an electric saw and cut ten inches around Butch to take him to the morgue as they found him. They lifted Butch still nailed to the wooden cutting table onto the stretcher and wheeled him out. The outline of Butch's body on the cutting table sent another shiver racing the length of my spine. One helluva way to go.

    With no further questions for us, Jones permitted us to leave. We stopped at Queenie's office on the way out of the factory. We tore the room apart, but her sweater had disappeared into thin air. Queenie was beside herself. The prized sweater meant the world to her.

****

    Queenie and I finally sat across from one another around nine at Pasta at the Pier, a local Marina Del Rey trattoria on Washington Street two blocks east of the beach. Queenie took a big gulp of her second scotch on the rocks and shook her head. "I don't think I'll ever sleep again. I'd be afraid to close my eyes." She shuddered. "I will never forget the image of Butch's corpse."

    I wiggled my eyebrows. "Which image bothered you more? Him wearing those ladies' panties or splayed out like one of his butterflies?"

    Queenie pinned me with a look capable of melting a steel beam. "The one with the shears planted in his chest, you dolt."

    I puffed the air out with my cheeks. "So, who do you think killed him?"

    Butch and his hand-picked partner in crime, Dick Green, our Chief Financial Officer, destroyed the company by draining it financially. The authorities caught Dick red-handed with two suitcases stuffed with company cash as he attempted to leave the country. Dick is currently sitting in jail awaiting an indictment sure to come down any day now. By the time the FBI gathered enough evidence against our CEO to put him in the cell next to Dick, Butch was dead. The two executives became the newest poster boys for those TV ads with the deputy dog who warns crime doesn't pay.

Queenie reminded me of my nana as she tapped the tip of her nose. "Dunno. With Butch's legion of fans, the line of suspects is gonna be mighty long. The only one not in the running is Dick Green, the current guest of the Fed's finest hospitality at the Graybar Hotel."

Nothing gets past you, Queenster.

Chapter Two

The next morning, David summoned every Mermaid employee to gather into the drafty factory lobby. Their concerned faces said, who's next? No kidding. The last time a company meeting called them together, Butch Oldham announced Mermaid Swimwear had filed for bankruptcy protection. More than half of the attendees left that confab unemployed. From their looks of resignation, they'd braced themselves for the worst. They waited for Butch to either announce the joint had closed down completely or, if they *were lucky*, just the next round of layoffs. And if it was the latter, which of them were now out of work?

As a pale, shaken David Workman and mum Mr. Smythe stood in front of them, the employees craned their necks looking for Butch. When it was obvious Butch wouldn't appear, they turned to one another with question marks in their eyes. Maybe the squirt finally got fired? He deserved it. Since the company went belly up, and the catastrophe happened on his watch, as CEO, he must be responsible.

David smiled wanly at the expectant faces. Queenie and I stood in the back and glanced at one another when David waved for quiet. This ought to be good. Who needs TV soap operas if you already star in one of your own? David cleared his throat three times before he choked out the words. "Ladies and gentlemen, it is with profound shock and sadness I must inform you of the unprovoked and violent murder of our beloved CEO."

I elbowed her in the ribs to shut her up when Queenie muttered loud enough for half the employees to hear, "I say good riddance. It couldn't happen to a better man. Whoever killed him deserves a reward."

David's voice quavered with emotion. "The industry has lost a great leader, and I've lost a mentor and dear friend." David swiped at his eyes. "Ladies and gentlemen, our Butch Oldham is dead."

Queenie leaned over and whispered, "Boy, he's good. David must be gagging on those words." Queenie puckered her lips. "Or, the more plausible scenario. David is putting on an Academy Award performance to cover his ass."

I gave her the big eyes. "You think he's acting? Why?"

Queenie tapped her index finger to the tip of her nose. "You don't cross David Workman and escape unscathed." She arched a brow. "It wouldn't surprise me in the least if it turns out David killed the rat."

I gave her the stink eye. "With the way you found Butch? You've got to be kidding. A bloody mess far too icky for our elegant boss to do the deed. David Workman gets his hands dirty? Not a chance."

At first, you could hear your pulse as everyone absorbed the news. Then the lobby buzzed as loud as an angry bee swarm that had escaped the hive. Not surprisingly, a fair share of smiles quirked amongst the shocked faces. Since Butch wasn't nominated by any employee for the boss of the year, not one of his employees shed a single tear for him. It would not surprise anyone if Butch's killer stood someplace in the crowd. David clapped once for quiet and the place appropriately turned silent as a tomb. "This is an irreplaceable loss for us all. Butch would want us to be strong and go forward together. The greatest tribute we can pay him is to continue working as a team to overcome the challenges we face." David seemed to shrink into himself as he swept an arm towards Mr. Smythe. "Mr. Smythe has a few thoughts to share with us."

The bespectacled Mr. Smythe smiled tightly at the group. "Thank you, Mr. Workman. During the coming days, perhaps even for a few weeks, the police will be on campus investigating this horrific crime. They will be interviewing many of us, perhaps several times. Please extend them your full cooperation. Answer their questions honestly and thoroughly. We must do everything possible to help them find the person or persons responsible for this evil act. As the investigation moves forward and uncovers the facts, we will be inundated with questions from the press, the industry, and individuals hoping perhaps to seize this time of great sadness and unrest at Mermaid to their advantage and use it against our company." Mr. Smythe gazed across the audience with his keen gray eyes. "Each of us is a representative of Mermaid, irrespective of the position we hold with the company. Let me caution you all to not make comments to or answer any questions regarding this situation with anyone other than the police."

Mr. Smythe held his bony left hand out like a traffic cop, as though the flow of potential questions could be stopped with the simple gesture. "Great pressure will be on you and frankly great temptation, to weigh in on this crime. To serve our best interests and out of respect for

Mr. Oldham, you must resist. Please say nothing, as your comments are liable to hurt rather than help the investigation and our company as well. If you are approached, please refer all questions to either me or Mr. Workman. Thank you for your cooperation."

And without uttering another word or allowing the employees to ask any questions, David and Mr. Smythe turned about-face and strode purposely out of the lobby. They left the employees standing looking at one another with a mixture of relief and fear etched on their faces. Some were just relieved they still had jobs. Others, fearfully searched their colleague's faces for clues as to which one of them was finally pushed past their limits and murdered Butch Oldham. The options were legion.

****

If Mermaid was the talk of the industry once we filed bankruptcy, that was fun and games compared to the frenzied reaction to Butch Oldham's murder. We'd all been instructed not to talk about the crime with anyone other than the cops. After three days of relentless questions from competitors to retailers to reporters, Queenie, David, and I stopped answering our phones. Holed up as a prisoner in my office, I stared at Butch's photo under the screaming headlines in the trade papers. As my wise nana always said, *nothing ever turns out the way you think it will*. No kidding. Just ask Butch and David.

Chapter Three

Halfway through my story, Joan Binder, Vice President of Sales at Royal Swimwear and the yappiest of the Yentas, sputtered. "Butterflies? Butch Oldham's murder? What in tarnation is the common denominator?"

Before Joan's interruption, I'd been relating that my heart had skipped a few beats when Detective Jones called the day before and asked if I would meet him in Butch's office. Good grief. Did my nutty, but uncontrollable burst of inappropriate laughter make me a suspect? My ticker resumed beating regularly when he explained that he might need some clarifications or answers to questions. Why he chose me? I dunno. But as long as handcuffs and an orange jumpsuit weren't in my future, I agreed to help.

I picked up the story at the place I'd left off. "He explained the methodology he used to approach a murder investigation. 'Like dancing the tango, it takes two to commit murder. You need a killer and the prey. To find the first you need an understanding of the second. Embedding myself in the victim's surroundings helps get me inside the victim's head.'"

I panned the Yentas to demonstrate how Jones looked around the neat as a pin orderly office. Not a paperclip on the floor, not a file on the desk. I surveyed the table. "It's weird the way the place looked. It was so clean; it was as if no one had ever worked in the office.

Butch wasn't a slob, but he never struck me as a neat freak either."

Mermaid juniors and kids' swimwear division president Sonia Wilson tilted her head. "You said the FBI was closing in on Butch, right?"

I nodded my agreement and she went on. "Maybe he sanitized the office? Shredded documents, took others out of the office? Maybe he wiped the place completely clean."

Joan arched a brow. "Or, the FBI raided Butch's office and grabbed anything not nailed down."

I shrugged. "Either scenario is plausible. Anyway, the detective's eyes focused on the butterfly collection housed in glass cases that were hung on the walls. He looked back and forth between the crime scene photos and the butterflies mounted in the glass cases. He pointed to the glass cases and spoke more to himself than to me. 'Not sure why, but I feel it in my gut. It's the common denominator and the key to solving the case. The way and why I don't exactly have figured out yet.' "

Joan shook her head. "I dunno. I don't see the connection between butterflies and Butch Oldham's murder." She shrugged. "Guess that's why he's the detective and I sell swimsuits."

I offered some details about Butch's collection. "Butch owned quite an impressive butterfly collection. He had a small one at his office and at one time, another, more extensive one decorated his home."

Ditzy Swimwear Showroom Manager Hope Greenberg dipped her head. "You said *at one time* he had the second collection. Was it sold or stolen or given away?"

I shook my head. "Nope. The collection was

vandalized during a house burglary. Most of the mounts were destroyed."

Hope grimaced. "Who would do such a mean thing?"

Joan puckered her lips. "My vote goes to the almost ex-wife."

I shook my head in agreement. "At the time of the incident, Butch voted for the wife too. But the police investigated, and no one was ever arrested. It's a shame. The collection took Butch years to amass, and it meant the world to him. His secretary, Helen, said he never got over the loss. Anyway, Jones finished studying the butterflies and re-examined the crime scene photos lying on the conference table. He studied the way Butch lay splayed on the cutting table on top of the fabric, as though he was the subject inside a framed picture. Jones was especially interested the way Butch was pinned to the cutting table and clad in ladies' panties with his dick hanging out. Every detail must be a clue to the killer's identity."

I picked up a knife and stabbed the remnants of my cheese Danish into a pile of crumbs. "This wasn't a murder. This was a rage killing. Whoever killed Butch wasn't satisfied just killing him. The killer wanted Butch humiliated as much as the killer wanted Butch dead." I snapped my fingers. "If Jones figures out why the killer was enraged enough to mount and display Butch like one of his butterflies, Jones will solve the murder."

Joan widened her eyes. "The detective's biggest problem won't be identifying suspects. It will be eliminating them from the legion of Butch Oldham's fans."

Sonia drummed a beat on the table. "So, which of

Butch's legion of fans killed him?"

Hope gave Queenie and me the big eyes. "Since it happened at the Mermaid warehouse, it had to be an inside job."

It was no state secret. Queenie and I both despised Butch. He was a traitorous slug who milked our company dry and destroyed it for personal profit. But good grief. Hope actually accused one of us as being the murderer? I restrained myself and resisted smacking her silly. It took an effort not to speak through clenched teeth. "Not necessarily. A cast of thousands of suppliers is at the factory daily. Fabric companies, trim companies, sewing contractors, and computer companies. Butch was an equal-opportunity scoundrel. He screwed them all."

Queenie tapped her index finger on the tip of her nose. "On TV the detectives always say to follow the money. Who has the most to lose?"

We chorused, "Kelly Oldham."

Joan asked, "And after her, who?"

I counted the victims on my fingers. "First, Harry O'Shea, Butch's fishing partner and the company's biggest investor. Then the Chairman of the board, Earl Bernard, and the other board members. All of them lost a bucket of bucks. And let's not leave out Dick and Mariana Green."

Sonia scrunched her nose. "Isn't Dick Green in jail?"

I nodded yes.

Hope said, "So, he's not the one who killed Butch. Last time I looked they don't let prisoners out of jail unless they're proven innocent."

Joan pursed her lips. "He stole millions. Maybe he hired someone to do the deed."

Sonia tapped her upper lip. "The police dropped the charges against the wife, so she's out of jail. Maybe she hired someone?"

I widened my eyes. "Mariana tells anyone who'll listen Butch set Dick up to take the fall. So, maybe she hated Butch enough to do the deed herself."

Joan raised an index finger. "David Workman gets my vote. Talk about a colossal betrayal. David brings Butch into the company after the little twirp gets fired from Royal, and the ungrateful rat shows his gratitude by stabbing David in the back and stealing his job."

Queenie hung her head. "Don't forget about me."

Imitating synchronized swimmers, the Yentas swiveled their heads to Queenie.

Joan pointed a teaspoon at Queenie. "Why you? Because you blamed Butch for destroying Mermaid? Pardon me all to hell, but who else *could* you blame?"

Queenie bunched her shoulders. "Butch and I go way back. Remember, he brought me to Royal Swimwear at the same time as David. It's ancient history and something I'm not proud of…" She had the grace to blush. "Stupid me. I made the mistake of falling for his BS and having an affair with him."

If they dropped any further, the Yentas' jaws would have hit the table.

Queenie snapped, "Hey, don't look at me so funny. Pretty amazing for a twenty-year-old newbie hoping to advance her career and presto, the CEO of the company seeks her out. Young, naïve, and stupid, I was flattered someone in his position took an interest in me. But," Queenie grinned. "To tell you the truth, I was kinda attracted to him."

Joan giggled. "Yikes. You were attracted to a troll?

How much more desperate can you get?"

Queenie jutted her jaw. "Hey, he wasn't *born* a troll. Back in the day, he was cute in a needy, nerdy kind of way." Queenie waved her hand dismissively. "Believe me, it only lasted a short time. We were an item for a few months until the new flavor of the season came along to take my place."

Sonia asked, "You discovered Butch dead on the cutting table, right?"

Queenie closed her eyes and shuddered as she nodded.

Sonia said, "Does the cop know about your history with Butch?"

Queenie huffed, "If he does, it wasn't from me. It's not exactly something I'm proud of."

Joan pursed her lips into a funnel. "It's way better for him to hear it from you than for you to hear it from him."

Joan's warning sent a shiver across my heart. Would it come back to haunt Queenie?

Chapter Four

Harriet Cowan had bleach-blonde, big hair and a Mae West-hourglass figure going to middle-aged lumpy plump. Fiftyish Harriet had been David's secretary for ten years. She bosses David around, not the reverse. He just doesn't realize it. Harriet runs the executive suite with the authority and precision of a marine drill sergeant. *Nothing* happens at Mermaid without Harriet's knowledge or sanction. If you want to get *anything* done at Mermaid, Harriet is the go-to girl.

Harriet's cramped office and David's massive one are attached by a pass-way with a split door. If someone sat at David's conference table, they couldn't see the pass-way. Queenie and I sat in with Harriet going over some figures when Detective Jones walked into David's office. Harriet put a shushing finger to her lips and cracked the pass-way open. The three of us jockeyed our positions until we stacked on top of one another like those Russian doll sets so as not to miss a word.

Jones sat across from David and smiled. "Mr. Workman thanks so much for seeing me again. I'll try to keep this as short as possible."

David nodded and Jones went on. "Tell me about your relationship with Mr. Oldham."

David beamed a hundred-thousand-watt smile. "Butch was my mentor and my friend. I credit him for my successful career. He plucked me out of a going-no-place retail buying position and brought me into the wholesale end of the industry. He took me under his wing at Royal Swimwear and taught me everything I know." David's voice cracked. "I owe him everything. I just regret not having the chance to repay him."

Jones tilted his enormous head to the side the same way my dog Siggie does if he's trying to understand something. "You more than repaid him. You brought Mr. Oldham to Mermaid after he got fired from Royal Swimwear."

David tipped his head and Jones scratched a note. Jones looked up from his notepad. "Weren't you the head honcho in charge here before Mr. Oldham joined Mermaid Swimwear?"

David took a few beats before he replied. "Butch's real strength was in operations and mine was in design and sales." David tried to smile, but it never reached his eyes. "Frankly, my operational skills weren't impressing the board of directors. I don't blame them. They weren't impressing me either." David laughed self-deprecatingly. "The rumor mill said the board considered shopping for a COO whose main job would be my minder. I thought it best to be proactive and bring in my own person, rather than wait for the board to shove some unknown down my throat."

Jones cocked a brow. "So, yours was a self-serving reason to bring Mr. Oldham to the company."

David pursed his lips. "I guess that's *one way* you could take it." David shrugged. "Look, the best man for the job just happened to be someone who worked out well for me too." David grinned. "Nothing wrong with a win-win, right?" David unconsciously pulled at his shirt collar as though it strangled him. More likely, he choked

Susie Black

on the lie he tried to peddle.

Jones leaned forward and invaded David's space with his huge body. "Mr. Workman, I don't think you've been completely honest with me about your relationship with Mr. Oldham."

David's head jerked back as though he'd been sucker-punched. "You must be crazy. I considered Butch a second father."

David's jaw bunched as the cop taunted him. "The pressure just gets to you and you stepped aside, or you woke up one morning and realized Mr. Oldham stole your job?"

David smacked his palm down hard on his desk and the crystal paperweight in the center rolled to the edge when he yelped. "Neither!"

Jones snickered. "So, I suppose you weren't the least bit upset after you brought him to Mermaid to watch your back, and instead Mr. Oldham went behind it, and stole your job right out from under you?" Jones shook his head. "Really, Mr. Workman. If that's your story, you're either a liar or a fool. Rest assured, I am no fool. Give me a real answer and not some cock and bull you pulled out of your ass."

David snapped. "Fine. The truth is, yes, I'd been betrayed." David took a controlling breath and grinned. "But in the end, it worked out dandy for me. The difference between Butch and me is he was all about power and control and image. I'm all about doing a job I love and money. M-O-N-E-Y: Lots of it. Believe me, when he became CEO, I cut myself one helluva sweetheart deal. In the end, we both got everything we wanted."

David smiled like the unscrupulous snake oil

24

pitchman we all knew him to be. "He got to be lord of the kingdom and I got my dream job and buckets of moolah. I hope you find whoever killed him. I'm sorry to disappoint you, but I'm not your guy." David stood up and glared at Jones as he pointed to the office door. "Now if you'll excuse me, I've got a company to run."

Chapter Five

The next morning Detective Jones and I danced an awkward do-see-dos with one another as I left David's office and the cop was on his way in. Jones left the door open, so, a nosy parker such as me, stood in the hallway and eavesdropped. I angled my body sideways. If I turned my head perpendicular to the floor, the completely cockeyed position gave me an unobstructed view of them, but not them a view of me.

The color drained out of David's face as Jones put his ham-sized hands on David's desk and leaned halfway over. "Mr. Workman, I'm afraid you weren't too honest with me the last time we spoke."

David reared back and snarled. "What the hell do you mean?"

Jones laughed a nasty laugh as he imitated David. "I *mean* you failed to share the dirty little secret Mr. Oldham held over your head. The one he threatened to expose to the industry and your family."

David shrugged away his indifference. "I've no idea what you're talking about."

Jones rolled his eyes. "I think you do. It's true that Mr. Oldham agreed to a great financial package for you after he stole your job. But isn't it a fact you blackmailed him into your new deal, and yet he still kept you under his thumb?" Jones waved a paw the size of a catcher's mitt in David's face. "He threatened to expose you as gay and out you to the world. Isn't it a fact he was homophobic and told you how much you disgusted him?" Jones framed his huge hands out in front of his body the way a movie director setting a scene does. "You confront him. You argue. He mocks you. Enraged, you look around for a weapon, anything to shut him up. You grab the first one you see and shove the fabric cutting shears into his chest."

David squealed with the high pitch of an embarrassed schoolgirl. "Have you lost your mind? I didn't blackmail him, confront, him, stab him, or kill him." David waved his dismissal away with a flick of a wrist. "As to my alleged outing? Such yesterday's news." David huffed. "An old rumor, and probably the worst kept secret in the industry. It's been going around for ages. And no one takes it seriously." David clucked like a hen. "I wasn't under his thumb over anything. If that's the best you've got, you're no place."

Normally cool under fire, David pulled a handkerchief out of his sportscoat pocket and nervously swiped at the beads of sweat dotting his forehead. Detective Jones smiled coldly. "It goes to motive Mr. Workman, and I've seen arrests stick with a lot less. I see you for this, Mr. Workman, so don't make any plans to leave town." Jones stood up and strode out of David's office. I scampered in the other direction as the cop went into Queenie Levine's office.

****

Queenie was angry enough to spit bullets as she paced back and forth in my office later in the afternoon. In case I missed it the first ten times she said it, she repeated it a few dozen more. "The nerve of the guy."

I let her pace and stew for a few minutes more and

then I said, "So, are you gonna tell me why your panties are in such a bunch or just keep pacing? Because if all you're gonna do is pace and stew, please tell me, so I'll go back to my project."

The intake of oxygen from her sigh almost sucked all the air out of the room, but she finally stopped pacing and spat the problem out.

I hid my amusement behind my coffee mug as my diminutive friend mimicked the gigantic cop. "Ms. Levine, I've re-read the statement you gave, but please tell me again in your own words the circumstances leading you to discover Mr. Oldham's body." Queenie rolled her eyes. "I resisted the urge to ask if this was some sort of quiz. I repeated for the *umpteenth* time I met with Holly Schlivnik and our head designer Gary Burkett. We were working together on product development for a program a retailer requested." Queenie puffed the air out with her cheeks. "You'd think my answer was enough." She sighed as though the weight of the world rested on her narrow shoulders. "But no, he waved me to go on." She spoke in a monotone, as though reciting from memory. "The two rolls of sample yardage I wanted for this program weren't in the design room. I remembered they were in the sample yardage bins in the warehouse. So, I went there to get them. They were on the top bins so I climbed up the ladder to get to them. I couldn't hold them both and get down off the ladder safely, so I let them drop to the ground. I got off the ladder and grabbed a pair of cutting shears, some eye pins to hold the fabric in place while I cut the swatches, and picked up the first roll. The second roll stuck out from under a cutting table, I bent down to pick it up. I stood up and faced the cutting table with Butch's body impaled on it. I screamed and dropped everything. I ran to the nearest phone and called Holly."

She said Jones scratched a note and asked, "The cutting shears and pins are the same as those found on Mr. Oldham?"

She said she nodded yes. She said he asked, "So these tools are commonly found in the warehouse?" She sighed and said she repeated the rest of the conversation. "Yes, they are *the* tools used to secure and cut sample yardage from the rolls." Queenie said Jones asked, "Do you use those types of tools regularly?" Queenie said she gave Jones an odd look. "Not just *me*. *Everyone* in the industry does."

Queenie said she explained the usual procedure. "Normally if I need a fabric swatch, I call the warehouse manager, give him the pattern number and the color I want the swatch cut in, and then a cutter in production cuts it for me. The warehouse opens at six in the morning and everyone is gone by three. I needed the swatches late afternoon. Everyone in the warehouse had already left, so I got them myself."

Queenie said Jones made a note and changed direction. "When you first discovered Mr. Oldham, did you make any attempt to help him? A normal reaction is to try to save someone. You said in your statement you never touched him or made any attempt to save him. Why not?"

Queenie imitated the bug-eyed expression of incredulity she gave the cop. "You're kidding, right? With cutting shears stuck in his chest?" Queenie snorted, "I'm no Doctor Welby, but it seemed pretty obvious he was beyond help."

She said Jones shrugged. "Ok fair enough. You

found Mr. Oldham. Why call Ms. Schlivnik and not 911?"

Queenie hiccupped a laugh. "I told him, gee Detective, I never experienced finding someone with shears in his chest before. Maybe next time I'll know the drill."

Queenie looked disappointed that Jones chose to ignore her sarcasm. He asked, "Please describe your relationship with Mr. Oldham."

Queenie shrugged. "I said I worked for him. And he asked if Butch was my direct supervisor. I said no, David Workman is my direct supervisor. Mr. Oldham was the CEO of the company, so technically, we all worked for him. Then he asked how long I'd known Butch and I said twelve years. He asked if we worked together before, or if I just knew him from being in the same industry? I said I worked for him many years before at Royal Swimwear." Queenie rolled her eyes. "He asked me to characterize my relationship with Butch."

To my surprise, she kept her normally smartass remarks to herself. "I told him, like any boss and employee, we had our ups and downs, agreements and differences of opinion, but overall, an ok relationship. Since he wasn't my direct boss, there wasn't much daily interaction between us."

Jones is no slouch. He'd done his homework. I doubted he took her at her word. I asked, "So, how'd Jones take it?"

Queenie sucked in her cheeks. "Jones gave me a hard look. He said it's common knowledge you blame Mr. Oldham for the company's bankruptcy. You provided documents to the FBI that led to their investigating him. You've been heard on several occasions saying he's responsible for Mermaid going bankrupt and…" she said he made quote marks with his sausage-sized fingers and said, "he's gonna get his." Queenie jutted her jaw. "I looked the cop in the eye and said, you're damned right I blamed Butch for Mermaid's demise. Yes, I gave those documents to the FBI. If anything, it proved I am a good citizen by contacting the FBI. *That's* how I thought he should get his."

Seemed reasonable to me. "So, he lightened up?"

Queenie gave me the stink eye. "Not on your life. Jones turned my words around. He said*, or you gave the documents to the FBI, but got frustrated when Mr. Oldham wasn't immediately arrested, and you took matters into your own hands*." Queenie shook her head in disbelief. "He said, Ms. Levine, you had both the motive and the opportunity."

Oh boy. It is not a brain surgeon move to push Queenie Levine around, even if you are a one-hundred-foot-tall cop packing a big ass gun. "To wit you replied?"

She squared her shoulders. "With all due respect detective, if you had one shred of hard evidence, I'd be under arrest already."

Yikes, Queenie. If it wasn't already in his mind, your suggestion did the trick. Way to antagonize the cop, Queenster. Visions of my pal sporting a bright orange jumpsuit and her wrists shackled by handcuffs danced inside my head.

Queenie said, "he said, I don't mind telling you Ms. Levine, I like you a lot for this murder. Mark my words, I'm working hard to close this one and your face keeps popping into my field of vision."

Queenie spat out the words as though they were pieces of a wormy apple. "I said, you're barking up the

31

wrong tree. It's true. I hated Butch. But I didn't kill him. Believe me, he had a legion of fans." Queenie laughed meanly. "I said, keep looking, detective. Don't be too surprised if you find plenty of candidates who hated Butch Oldham a helluva lot more than me."

Queenie may have won the skirmish, but she lost the war. She did herself no favor by smart-mouthing Detective Jones.

Chapter Six

The life-size color photograph of Butch Oldham resting on a large easel in the middle of a raised dais stood twice as tall as Butch in real life. He still looked the same as a Humpty Dumpty, only now one on drugs. An elaborate, oversized marble urn with gold leaf flower-shaped fleur d' les handles sat on a tall, narrow table next to the photo. Surrounded by gorgeous floral arrangements, the ostentatious urn held the last of the earthly remains of Benjamin "Butch" Oldham. The photograph and urn were placed in front of the first row of mourners and adjacent to a lectern. Four sets of spotlights aimed at the photograph featuring Butch Oldham all decked out in a snazzy tuxedo. Humpty Dumpty has gone formal. Butch smiled arrogantly down on the capacity crowd of mourners packed inside the mortuary chapel. Even in death, Butch Oldham still knew the way to work a room.

Butch's adult children and ex-wife were dressed in black and seated together on the left side of the chapel in the front row on the right end. Kelly and her "friend" Diane sat together directly across from the first family on the right side of the chapel in the front row on the left end. The modern-day version of the Hatfields versus the McCoys glared at one another.

The Mermaid employees sat together in the back two rows. Queenie and I sat next to one another in the two seats closest to the exit. Queenie pointed at Butch's photo. "My God, check out Butch's photo. Humpty Dumpty goes to the prom." Queenie giggled, "Too bad the photo didn't feature him in those lacy ladies' underpants."

I clamped a fist over my mouth as a vision of Butch in those panties inserted itself in my brain. I made the universal cut across the throat sign to shut Queenie up. Fanfreakingtastic. I needed a comedienne to help me along like I needed a hernia. When Queenie cracked her joke, I naturally looked up and made the mistake of glancing at Butch's picture. I tried stifling my giggles. As if. I sputtered like a car engine with faulty spark plugs with a snort that came out someplace between a cough and a laugh.

Queenie rolled her eyes. "Do you have a hanky or something? Or should I just keep my hand over your mouth for the rest of the service?"

I shot her my fiercest death ray glare. Hopefully, she got the hint. Oh sure. To be on the safe side, I waved at the aisle bisecting the two sides of the chapel. "Switch seats with me. Let me sit on the end. I might need to run out if I can't control myself." I angled my head at Butch's photo and sniffed with righteous indignation. "You were raised better than that. No matter how much you hated him, you shouldn't speak ill of the dead."

Queenie wrinkled her nose as if she'd taken a whiff of yesterday's garbage. "Why be a hypocrite? Nothing's changed. If you're an asshole all your life, you're still an asshole in death." Queenie pointed to the urn. "Talk about tacky? It's something one of those billionaire sheiks pick to decorate their mega-mansions with on Rodeo Drive."

I hiccupped a laugh. "Butch took the "ashes to ashes" line a bit too literally," I whispered through my guffaws. "I'll bet the murderer is thrilled Butch's body was toasted to dust. No way to dig him up in case the cops find something later and need to confirm it."

Queenie reminded me of my Nana as she tapped the tip of her nose. "I hadn't thought of that, but you're right." Queenie dipped her head at Butch's two wives. "They probably fought over who got the pleasure of striking the match."

I deadpanned. "Gee, I wonder whose mantle Butch is gonna decorate? They might have to draw straws to be fair."

Queenie snickered. "If you ask me, they ought to flush him down the toilet like a dead goldfish. It's the most fitting end to the miserable bastard."

The choice was either to burst a gut or burst out laughing. I chose door number two. Queenie put her hand over my mouth. I resisted the urge to bite her. Two old lady mourners in the row in front of us turned around to express their disapproval with a cluck of their tongues followed by self-righteous glares. I responded by sticking my tongue out and favoring them with the middle finger salute. Geesh, can't anyone take a joke?

****

Sophie Cutler swallowed a huge bite of pizza and grinned. "So, I guess you couldn't control yourself at the funeral." She used her greasy fingers to wipe off some pizza sauce dribbling down the side of her mouth. "Good thing you weren't giving the eulogy."

Who says coroners are devoid of a sense of humor? I gave her my best shit-eating grin. No use denying it. My pal knew me too well. "Thank God for small favors.

Between Queenie's wisecracks and jokes, I never stood a chance." I narrowed my eyes. "You weren't at the funeral. So, who spilled the beans?"

She licked the pizza sauce off her fingers with a flourish. "No, I wasn't, but I got a blow-by-blow description of your antics from Detective Jones."

I blushed from head to toe and slunk down low in my seat.

"He stood right behind you and Ms. Levine." Sophie rolled her eyes. "Sounds as if you guys put on quite a performance. He expressed quite a bit of interest in the conversation you two had." My heart skipped a beat as she smirked. "Let's just say Ms. Levine didn't help herself. From Jones' description, after her antics, she's moved up the list to his number one suspect."

I speared Sophie with a look strong enough to strip the first two layers of paint off my vintage sixty-five bubblegum pink convertible. "Oh, come on. Not one single person in the chapel was there to *mourn* Butch Oldham. A mob of looky-loos showed up out of morbid curiosity. And considering they're going to inherit a fortune from him, even his children shed no tears for their dear, departed, daddy."

Sophie smirked. "Be that as it may, but only *one mourner,* specifically, the divine Ms. Levine, suggested flushing the victim's remains down the toilet as a fitting burial."

I waved the point away as though it was an annoying gnat. "It's true. Queenie hated Butch. And she blames him for Mermaid's troubles. Believe me, it's easy to name a cast of thousands who hated him just as much if not more."

Sophie huffed with indignation. "Hey, I'm just the

corpse cutter. I'm not the one she has to convince."

Queenie needed an ally who Jones trusted. I nominated Sophie. "Queenie is innocent. Help me prove it."

Snip grabbed another slice of pizza and chomped a huge bite before she responded. "From the autopsy, we found no physical evidence linking Ms. Levine to the murder."

I tsked. "Come on. Ya gotta give me something more than that."

Snip daintily dabbed her lips with a napkin and then waved it at me. "Listen, Nancy Drew, if I do, you *must* promise not to play amateur sleuth and interfere with the detective's investigation. The last time you stuck your nose into an investigation, you almost got yourself killed."

Indeed. Snip didn't exaggerate, so, regrettably, it did no good to argue the point. Butch Oldham's was not my first corpse. Actually, several preceded his. And much to my chagrin, a couple of times, I came perilously close to losing my life. "Hey, it's not as if I roused myself out of bed one morning and said, "Gee, today might be a great day to see how far I can go without getting myself killed. Shit happens. Unfortunately, a lot of the time, shit seems to happen to me."

My dear lifelong friend Sophie Cutler rolled her eyes.

Queenie Levine as the culprit who killed Butch? The thought was laughable. She was incapable of killing a cockroach. She would cringe and say it was "*too icky*," for crying out loud. Queenie Levine is my friend. I won't sit on my hands and let Jones lock her up and throw away the key. I jutted my jaw. "Help me or not, but you can go to the bank on it that I'm gonna do this anyway. She's innocent. She's my friend, and she'd do the same for me." I gave Sophie my most pathetic hangdog look as I crossed my fingers behind my back and prayed not to be punished for all my lies. "The best I can do is promise to try and stay out of Detective Jones' way."

Sophie sighed with resignation. "I'm gonna live to regret this. No question about the cause of death. The blade tip punctured the aorta and death was virtually instantaneous. He bled out in a matter of minutes. An injection site was found on the right side of his neck. The tox report indicated he was injected with a skeletal muscle relaxant someplace else first and then moved to the cutting table."

I asked, "Injected with the stuff like you take if you overdo it at the gym?"

Snip shook her head. "Nope. Regular muscle relaxants are mainly prescribed for muscle spasms. *Skeletal* muscle relaxants are drugs that block the neuromuscular junction. The process leads to paralysis of all skeletal muscles, starting with the small muscles of the face and ultimately paralyzing the diaphragm. Paralytic drugs temporarily interfere with the messages nerves send to the skeletal muscles of the body. The skeletal muscles are those which control movements of the face, arms, legs, back, and trunk. The diaphragm muscles which help expand the lungs are also paralyzed by these medications. While under the effect of a neuromuscular blocking agent, you would need mechanical assistance to help you breathe, because diaphragmatic muscle paralysis prevents you from breathing on your own. Paralytic drugs are rapidly distributed throughout the body once they are injected.

They quickly bind to and block neuromuscular binding sites on muscles to prevent them from functioning. Paralytic drugs are medications commonly given during surgery along with anesthesia so the patient doesn't move during a procedure and injure himself. Common ones include succinylcholine, rocuronium, vecuronium, mivacurium, cisatracurium, and atracurium."

I asked, "So unless the killer is a doctor or a pharmacist, how could he or she get their hands on such a drug?"

Snip said, "The killer had some knowledge of these types of drugs, access to a prescription pad, and a pharmacist loosey-goosy with the way he or she filled them."

I dipped my head. "Maybe the killer used a muscle relaxant prescribed for spasms, but increased the dosage to a lethal level?"

Snip wrinkled her brow. "Possibly. If a product containing botulinum toxin is used at a lethal level, for example, breathing would be impacted, but the victim could still move. The condition of Mr. Oldham's musculature proved he had been paralyzed. So, in this case, it is quite doubtful the killer injected a muscle relaxant for easing spasms into the victim's neck."

I winced as she described Butch's last moments of life.

"Since he was not under anesthesia, Mr. Oldham lay paralyzed, but conscious when he was killed. He couldn't move, scream, nor ultimately breathe once his diaphragm became paralyzed. He helplessly watched the killer torment him and then end his life. The killer positioned the victim in a very specific manner. Whoever killed him put some thought into it, and I'd say made one helluva statement."

Dr. Cutler wiggled her brows. "One other interesting, but not necessarily relevant thing is the victim had sex not long before he died."

Eek. I snorted. "Guess he went out with a bang." The good news? That tidbit might be the key to eliminate Queenie Levine from the detective's suspect list. Or, it could just mean the detective says the killer and lover are not one and the same.

Chapter Seven

Queenie stormed into my office. "You're not gonna believe this, but Detective Jones just called and asked permission to search my house. He said he could get a search warrant, but it looks better if I'd give the ok voluntarily."

The question is whether she'd dug in her heels or done the smart thing? "So, you said ok, or told him to get a search warrant?"

She shrugged. "I gave my permission. Forcing him to go to court for a search warrant only makes me look guilty of whatever it is he thinks I'd be hiding. I've no idea what he expects to find, but I've nothing to hide. I told him to knock himself out."

****

Sigmund is a social guy and Queenie is one of his best buds. To accommodate my hound who insisted on joining us for dinner, we chose the Lobo Cantina, one of our favorite hangouts with a dog-friendly outside patio. We warmed our hands around gaily painted ceramic coffee mugs as the cold onshore wind blew in. My pooch settled in under our table halfway between Queenie and me. The wind picked up, rustling the awning. I reached down to give him a love pat as my big boy stretched out and laid on both sets of our feet to keep us warm. A woman's best friend indeed.

Queenie and I gorged ourselves silly on the Mexican

lobster and enchiladas special. Stuffed to the gills, I resisted the urge to loosen the belt on my jeans a couple of notches at the table. We strolled on the Washington Street pier trying to walk our dinner off. Ha. We could probably walk to San Francisco, and I'd still need to loosen my belt. I better demonstrate some control next time. Maybe eat several hundred fewer tortilla chips for starters. As if. Not a chance. I'm just a Mexican food ho' at heart.

We stopped to watch one of the fishermen haul in a good-sized catch flopping around on the pier. Sigmund curiously stuck his snout into the murky ocean water after the fisherman put the doomed fish in a dented plastic bucket. Queenie pointed to the fish and said, "I can relate."

I glanced at the fish in the bucket and hunched my shoulders. "I ate dinner with Snip last night. She released the autopsy results to the detective and he's probably given them to Kelly by now." I slid my eyes over to Queenie. "Detective Jones stood right behind us at the funeral." I giggled despite the seriousness of the situation. "He heard our entire conversation, including your helpful suggestion for someone to flush Butch's remains down the toilet. Jones told Snip all about it."

Queenie groaned loudly, and it wasn't from over-eating "Freaking fabulous. Between the goldfish joke and my comments regarding the photo and the urn, I buried myself even deeper."

I snorted a laugh. "Suffice it to say, the detective is not your biggest fan. I hate to say it, but according to Snip, you're now his number one suspect."

Queenie flinched as though I'd slapped her. "No big shock. He gave me the same impression. By any chance, were the autopsy results shared with you?"

I tried to convey the gruesome details of the way Butch died, but the words stuck in my throat. It's not that I thought she couldn't take it. On the contrary. I feared she'd enjoy his suffering too much. Instead, I said, "Reluctantly, but yes. The cause of death is a punctured aorta. She also found an injection site on Butch's neck. He'd been drugged with some kind of powerful muscle relaxant and moved to the cutting table."

Queenie sighed. "Well, it certainly explains the detective's reaction to finding my Celebro."

I dipped my head. "What explains what?"

"They searched my house and found my Celebro. I use it if I'm sore after Pilates."

And? "Ok, so…?"

Queenie tried to put up a good front, but the fear in her voice betrayed her with a bitter laugh. "He suggested that I do not make any plans to leave town." Queenie stopped walking and waggled a finger. "Celebro is taken *orally*, not with a syringe. You'd think this eliminated me, but who knows with this cop? He seems so sure I killed Butch, he'd probably say I mashed the pills, added water, and injected it. Since he discovered I use muscle relaxants, he's probably working 24/7 to find something else to physically link me to this." Her voice cracked. "I'll probably be arrested any day now."

I'd be pooping in my panties by then if I walked in her shoes. Since such a revelation wouldn't raise her comfort level, I went with cautious optimism. "The muscle relaxant isn't helpful, but it's no smoking gun. Celebro isn't the only one on the market. From the way Snip described it, Celebro isn't the type of muscle relaxant used on Butch. Snip is working to identify the exact one used. Even if Celebro is the one, you're not the only person in LA using it. If he had anything more concrete, you'd be sitting in jail by now." I smiled slyly. "Snip told something else kinda creepy, but it might help you a lot."

Queenie yelped, "Well out with it already! I could use some good news. Orange is not my best color."

"WOOF, WOOF." My hound concurred.

I grinned goofily like a circus clown. "Butch had sex not long before he died." I laughed, "As I told Snip, guess Butch went out with a bang so to speak."

Queenie's shriek probably shattered every eardrum on the pier. "Fabulous news! I can't imagine who the lucky lady is, but we can eliminate *me* from the running!"

Sigmund barked a big "WOOF" of agreement.

I sighed. "Not to be a Debbie Downer, but Jones could say just because you didn't screw Butch, it doesn't mean you didn't kill him. All it might prove is that the killer and lover aren't the same person."

The sun slipped into the abyss of the horizon and another onshore wind blew in off the ocean. I shivered farther into my jacket as the cold, salty air blew over the pier railing and bit my face. Or the deadly serious conversation caused my shivers. Flip a coin. Chilled to the bone, I pulled my jacket tighter. Queenie is in trouble. I couldn't sugar coat it. "So far, it's circumstantial, but according to my friend AJ, many get arrested on a lot less. Jones seems to have focused all his attention on one person. *You.* The only way he'll consider another suspect is if someone else becomes a helluva lot more compelling. Since he's zeroed in on you, it's up to us to investigate and deliver the real killer."

Queenie is no pushover. She won't go down without a fight. "You're right, we've no choice." She put her game face on. "Ok, if I am Detective Jones, I'd investigate two other major suspects besides me. Kelly and David are the two with the most motive. David wins in the means and opportunity categories. But Kelly hated Butch the most. So, she wins hands down in the motive derby." Queenie touched her manicured index to the tip of her nose. "Kelly has a ginormous motive. She couldn't match Butch in the conniving department. He would cheat her out of a settlement, so she had nothing to lose. Maybe she arrived earlier, met him in his office, and screwed his brains out hoping to soften him up. Then she killed him after he still refused to cough up on the settlement."

Queenie grimaced at the memory. "Splaying him like one of his butterflies could only be done by someone close enough to him to realize the significance. Someone who wanted to humiliate him as well as make him pay with his life." Queenie glanced at me. "Remember, by the time you ran into Kelly, the receptionist, Butch's secretary, most of the office staff, and the warehouse crew already left for the day. If Kelly timed it right, she could have killed Butch, and no one was around to see her do the deed."

I nodded my agreement. "Detective Jones has probably focused on you three. Looking closer at David and Kelly is a given. But we've got to look at others who are more under the radar as well." I gave Queenie my best salesman I-can-do-anything smile. "I don't think we should discount anyone yet. Not even Dick Green. He could arrange Butch's death if he tried hard enough. And if not him, certainly his wife. As well as a legion of candidates who hated our vaunted leader enough to kill him."

Queenie warmed to the concept of multiple suspects. "All true. Almost everyone has access to a muscle relaxant. But finding out who has access to a syringe narrows the suspect list down. Let's walk back to my place and make a list of everyone we should investigate."

I stopped walking and laughed. "Whoa! There aren't enough hours in the day if we tried to investigate *everyone* with a motive to do Butch harm. We'd better cull the list down to the ones with either the most to lose or the ones he harmed the most. Since you knew him better than I, you compile the suspect list. While you're doing that, I'll call Snip and ask if she identified the exact muscle relaxant found in Butch. I'm also gonna ask her if it's possible to identify Butch's sex partner by her DNA. Maybe we'll get lucky and it'll be the same woman who killed him."

We reached the end of the pier and split up. Queenie went south on Speedway and Siggie and I headed two blocks east to Palawan Way. As we walked, I fired up my cell phone and called my favorite ME. "Snip, it's Holly. I imagine you're up to your elbows, so I'll make it quick. Just a couple of questions: One: Is the exact muscle relaxant you found in Butch's system identified? Two: Is it possible to identify Butch's last sex partner from the DNA?" I laughed out loud. "Believe me, it isn't Queenie. But whoever it is might be the killer too."

My friend's smile wafted through the phone. "Oh boy, this is just wonderful. I foolishly give you a few tidbits and you morph back into Nancy Drew." Then

Sophie's voice turned serious. "Holly, I warned you once and I'll warn you again. Do not stick your nose into this. Leave this to the pros. Josiah Jones will serve my head on a platter if you interfere and he figures out who gave you the information."

I resisted the urge to stomp my feet like a toddler, but not the whine out of my voice. "Come on! I just asked two questions. Humor me, please, Snip. It's important. Queenie's life is on the line."

Sophie backpedaled, or maybe she just threw in the towel. With a persistent personality combined with a stubborn streak a mile long like mine, I *can be* extremely annoying and hound her till she gave in. "Ok, ok." She sighed. "Question one: I am still working on identifying the exact muscle relaxant. Question two: Yes, if something exists in the system to compare it to." I laughed at the resolve in her voice. "You've reached your limit. No more questions. I mean it. Go back to selling swimsuits."

I gushed, "Snip, you're the best." I pushed the envelope. "So, you'll run the DNA through the system to see if you get any hits? How fast do you think you'll get the drug and DNA information?"

Snip moaned. "Goodbye."

I laughed, "If you don't ask you don't get. Stay in touch. Don't be a stranger now." She snorted as I sang offkey. "Call me, don't be afraid to just call me. Call me, and I'll be around."

Doc Death begged like a pauper. "*Enough already*! I'm hanging up now. The next sound you'll hear is a dial tone." The phone buzzed a loud dial tone into my ear. Guess I pushed the envelope too far.

Chapter Eight

I sat in the car for a couple of minutes to work up enough courage to ring Dick Green's doorbell early the next morning. This seemed a much better idea when Queenie and I divided up the names of suspects to interview. I'd taken Mariana, Dick's wife, because Dick inexplicably chose *me* to send a dossier of documents to via his attorney. Why Dick chose me as his carrier pigeon, I'll never know. Other than exchanging polite greetings in the hallway, I doubt I'd spoken a hundred words to the guy.

I trusted his lawyer no more than I trusted Dick, so I asked my Uncle Barry, himself an attorney, to check the guy out. The attorney turned out to be legit. But I was uncomfortable meeting Dick's lawyer by myself, so my uncle agreed to accompany me. Uncle Barry and I met at the Nosh N' Nibble deli on Beverly Drive for a bite before meeting with Dick's lawyer, whose office was down the street from the restaurant.

Concerned about my future at a bankrupt company, my uncle asked if anyone bought Mermaid. I shook my head no. Lots of looky-loos, but no buyers. He dipped a shoulder. "Why don't you buy it?" I choked on my coffee. Whatever he'd been smoking must be mighty strong.

He asked a few dozen questions, jotted some numbers on a napkin, and tapped the bottom figure with the cap of his pen. "If you're able to come up with half of this, I know a couple of guys."

My nana left each of her grandchildren a tidy sum. Uncle Barry invested mine, and I'd done quite well. But the total wasn't close to half the figure scribbled on the napkin. At best, I might be able to come up with one-third… if I reduced eating to every other day. Besides, who's kidding who? Even if I came up with all the money, me capable of running an entire company on my own? As if. Uncle Barry shrugged. "So, get yourself a couple of partners." Mental head slap. Of course. And fortunately, the perfect two worked only a few offices down the hall from mine.

While independent Queenie insisted on working to pay her own way through college, she came from money. Mermaid head designer Gary Burkett's life partner is an extremely successful stage-set designer. Remarkably, Queenie and Gary were keen on my proposal. After a half-dozen meetings with my uncle's two guys and a mountain of paperwork later, we presented our offer to Mr. Smythe and the bankruptcy court. A decision was expected any day now. Gulp. If the offer is accepted, would Nana approve of the way I used my inheritance? Her voice whispered inside my head. "Regret is the worst human emotion." Yeah, she'd be good with it.

The paperwork trail Dick Green provided didn't clear the disgraced CFO, but it incriminated Butch Oldham up to his eyeballs. Queenie and I turned all those documents over to the FBI, along with a copy of the ledger we found in Butch's desk drawer. The way we ended up with the ledger? Don't ask. You don't want to know. It took the FBI almost a month, but based on the evidence we gave them, they investigated Butch's involvement in Mermaid's demise. They interviewed Butch twice and were preparing to take him down, but his killer beat them to the punch.

Since I started nosing around to see if either Dick or his wife killed Butch, my bravado turned to mush. Miss Marple's reproach moved onto the passenger seat next to Siggie as I fiddled with the radio stations buying myself some time to put my big girl panties on and confront Mariana Green. I squared my shoulders and told Miss M "ok, fine, I'm going," as her frail hands pushed me towards Dick Green's front door. I tossed two *"I'm sorry you have to stay in the car"* treats to my pooch, cracked the window, and locked the door.

I bit my lip to conceal my reaction when Mariana Green opened the door to the modest Spanish-style one-story house located on a narrow, secluded street off Coldwater Canyon midway between Beverly Hills and the San Fernando Valley. She'd aged a decade since the company Christmas party. Already a short woman, she stood hunched and stooped over. It was as though her body had shrunk into itself and given up the fight. Her death warmed-over skin tone matched the pasty gray of wet cement. Her dark eyes sunk deep in their sockets. She resembled a cadaver as they searched my eyes with the haunted look of doomed prey. Mariana looked worse than Butch with those shears impaled in his chest. Butch had a good excuse for the shitty way he looked. Mariana? The walking dead, but too numb to lie down.

I stifled a giggle as she led me into the living room. Every chair and sofa were covered with clear plastic the same way several of my nana's friends protected their furniture. Freeze your tush off in the winter, and stick to the plastic in the summer. I sunk in up to my neck on the squishy sofa. The tips of my toes lacked a good twelve inches from the floor. Good grief. Sleuthing is gonna be pretty tough to pull off if I couldn't get off the couch.

I eyed the china tea service on the coffee table and inwardly groaned. I am strictly a coffee drinker. I hate tea. Give my share to the English. I only drink the swill if I'm sick. Without asking if I wanted any, Mariana poured a cup and handed it to me. I wasn't raised in a barn, so I took the tea and sipped. I'm still not a fan. It tasted bitter as burnt toast, but at least it was hot.

Mariana graced me with the ghost of a smile. "I must admit, your call surprised the heck out of me." She choked out a brittle laugh. "Dick is a pariah at Mermaid. I never expected to hear from anyone at the company except for more hate mail."

My jaw dropped. "Hate mail? You've gotta be kidding." On second thought, why be surprised? Dick Green hurt a lot of people and ruined many lives.

Mariana took a sip of tea and grimly smiled. "I wish. You'd be amazed. After the charges against me were dropped and I got released from jail, the phone rang off the hook day and night. I couldn't answer it for all the crank calls. Some were horrible and more than a few quite threatening. I changed the phone number and made it unlisted, but the calls continued. I gave the numbers to the police. They considered the calls threatening enough to post a patrol car out front for a week. Once the surveillance ended, I went to my sister in San Diego. I wasn't safe in my own home. My sister suggested selling the house and moving. And I'm considering it. I won't live in fear for the rest of my life."

Mariana's lucky all she got is only hate mail and crank calls. Dick's crimes were common knowledge and his address is not difficult to find out. A disgruntled employee let go due to the bankruptcy could easily throw a Molotov cocktail into the house. Dick might be innocent until proven guilty in the eyes of the law. But in the court of public opinion, Dick Green was already tried and convicted.

Mariana's red-rimmed obsidian eyes shone with unshed tears. "Dick says you're a straight shooter and fair-minded."

The blush of embarrassment heated my neck. Given the reason for my visit, the praise was undeserved.

She appraised me over the teacup rim. "To be blunt, why are you here?"

Why indeed. I tried not to gag at the words. Faking sincerity is not one of my strong suits. "To check if you and Dick are doing ok." According to my mother whenever I fibbed, I wore something she called my lying face. From Mariana's reaction, I guess I donned it then. If Mariana raised her eyebrows any higher, they'd disappear into her hairline. I went with a version of the truth if you squinted. "Look, I won't say I'm not upset by the things I've heard Dick is accused of doing, but not many of us believe he did it all on his own. It doesn't make him less guilty, but most people think he was directed."

Dick's wife might have blindly defended her husband, but to her credit, Mariana's take on Dick hit the target with a bullseye. "Dick is no mindless robot, but he's no mastermind either. He did *nothing* on his own." She smiled sardonically. "Dick was the one driving the bus, but Butch is the one fueling the engine. When Dick outlived his usefulness, Butch threw my husband under the bus and kept going. Butch Oldham destroyed

Mermaid Swimwear and destroyed our lives along with the company. I shed not a single tear over his death." The coldness of her tone chilled my tea. "The bastard got everything he deserved." She'd get no argument from me. Add Mariana Green to the list of another one of Butch Oldham's legions of fans.

With no intelligent response in mind, bitter though it tasted, the tea proved a welcome diversion. I finished off the swill and put the empty cup on the coffee table. A copy of *The Argonaut*, the throwaway paper distributed in the marina, lay open next to the tea service. The freebie paper reported local news of interest to boaters and posted a large classified section in the back. I picked up the paper and asked, "You own a boat?"

Mariana sighed as though she bore the weight of the world on her shoulders. "Unfortunately, yes."

"Power or sailboat?"

Mariana smiled tightly, "Blue Bay forty-four-foot cabin cruiser with twin diesel engines."

I whistled. "Wow, that's some boat. At the last LA boat show, the Blue Bay exhibit was packed while a lot of the other manufacturers sat around in empty booths playing cards out of boredom. I bet Blue Bay is giving some of the old-line manufacturers a run for their money. Where is she moored?"

"Porto Paloma Marina."

I turned a doubletake. "No kidding? My houseboat is moored in the same marina. Have you guys been in the marina long? What basin are you in?"

She said, "Six years this past June on the west side of the marina facing the entrance to the main channel. Across from the last of the three apartment buildings bisecting the two sides of the marina." Mariana sucked in her cheeks. "*By The Numbers* is moored in the next to last basin on the west side two in from the security gate."

I said, "I'm on the east side of the marina across from the first apartment building. We are at opposite ends, so I guess it's no surprise we haven't run into one another in the marina itself. But even so, it's kind of funny I've never seen you guys anyplace in Marina del Rey. I've been in the marina for over five years. Not in a restaurant, a market, or the marine supply. You out on the boat often?"

She stabbed a bony finger into her cleavage. "Me? Not on your life. Dick is the sailor in our family. If he isn't in the garage fiddling around under the hood of his precious gull-wing classic, he is on the boat. But me?" Mariana grimaced as though she ate a plate of bad clams and had a stomach cramp. "I'm strictly a landlubber." Mariana took an imaginary swing of a golf club. "I'm the golfer in the family." Every once in a while, I'll stick my nose under the hood of the gull-wing while Dick is working on it, but I only went aboard the boat under duress. The salt air is hell on my complexion. The waves make me queasy. And it takes me hours to get the knots out of my hair from the wind. Unless we entertained someone important and I was forced to make a command appearance, I wouldn't be caught dead on the damned floating money pit."

Entertaining? It was impossible to wrap my head around the concept of droll Dick Green as a bring-on the bubbly party animal. The humorless, bespectacled pencil pusher wore a complexion, personality, and wardrobe as dull and colorless as an undertaker.

Mariana narrowed her eyes. "Do you shop at Coast Marine Supply?"

I shrugged. "Where else?"

She gave me the big eyes. "Then it's a miracle you ever missed running into Dick." She demonstrated her disgust with a cluck of her tongue. "Coast Marine Supply is his home away from home."

I scratched my chin. "You called the boat a money pit. Dick went to Coast Marine Supply to fix problems on the boat?"

She rolled her eyes. "Hardly. He kept the boat in pristine condition."

I said, "I only go to Coast Marine Supply if I need something. It's not exactly a place to hang out at." I joked, "They start serving cheese and wine or something?"

She smirked. "No need. Dick is a willing stooge. Oh, Freddy, the manager is a sharp one. He saw a sucker the first time Dick walked into the store. Every time some new doohickey or gizmo came in, fast Freddy called Dick. Believe me, my husband didn't miss a single new thingamabob. You can't imagine the huge amount of money he pissed away on useless crap." She snarled. "The cleats on my golf shoes might be falling off, but he would pitch a fit if I dared say I needed a new pair. But for his precious boat? There was *no bottom* to that pit." Mariana picked up the paper and opened it to the classified ads. She turned the paper around to face me so I could see a bold-face-type-half-page ad with a color photo as well as the details of her boat for sale.

I'm no expert on the going prices for yachts, but for her class boat, Mariana's asking price was way below how much it was worth. "I hope you don't mind my saying, but you're practically giving the boat away. A boat like yours in pristine condition sells for a much higher price. Maybe you ought to pull the ad and re-price it. If you increased the price by forty percent, I bet your phone would still be ringing off the wall with offers. Your financial situation is none of my business, but I've gotta believe the extra money would come in handy right now."

Mariana closed the paper with a snap. "The upkeep and slip fees could choke a horse, but it's not why I priced it so low. Bottom line? I need the boat gone. Now. Tonight is not soon enough."

I narrowed my eyes. "Why the big rush?"

Mariana wrung her hands. "Cash is king and I need as much as I can get my hands on right now. I need some breathing room while I figure out my next move. The boat, our cars, and the house thank God, are all free and clear. But Dick's legal fees wiped out everything we saved, including a nest egg for retirement, and it still isn't enough." She held up her left hand and wiggled her ring finger. "I've already sold the gull-wing as well as all my good jewelry, except for my wedding band. I haven't worked in twenty years and have no marketable skills, so a job is out as a solution. Dick cut a deal with the Feds. He's going to do substantial time, but at least he'll be at a Club Fed, not a penitentiary." Her laugh turned bitter as a lemon wedge. "He has no need for a fancy boat or car at the place he's going to."

Mariana held the teapot up, but before she offered me a second cup, I smiled sheepishly and looked around. If I could haul myself off the sofa, the time had come to check out the house. "Mariana, excuse me, but may I use your little girls' room?" I shrugged and laughed self-deprecatingly. "Little girl, little bladder."

Mariana smiled and pointed. "No problem. Take a

right and you can't miss it at the end of the hallway."

After about a half dozen embarrassing tries, I managed to launch myself out of the couch. By then I wasn't lying. I had to pee. I walked by Mariana's cluttered desk. A World-Wide Gym monthly statement jutted out on the bottom corner.

I locked the bathroom door and quickly went through the drawers and medicine chest. Nothing but toiletries in the drawers. The first shelf in the medicine chest housed over-the-counter medications: Aspirin, Tylenol, cough syrup, and such. The second shelf held prescription medications for both Dick and Mariana. The bottle of valium with a few tablets in it prescribed to Mariana grabbed my attention. I took the bottle out and read the instructions. Adult dosage to manage anxiety. 10 mg. 2x daily: 1 pill AM 1pill PM. CAUTION: Drowsiness is a side effect. Avoid driving 5-7 hours after taking. I'm no psychologist, but Mariana's anxiety level seemed off the charts. No kidding. If I went through her recent experiences, I'd be popping my share of happy pills too. I put the bottle back on the shelf, finished my business, flushed the toilet, and closed the powder room door behind me.

The phone on the desk rang as Mariana walked me to the door. "Maybe I'll luck out and somebody's calling about the boat ad. What basin are you in? I'll be down at the boat in a few days to clean it out. Maybe we can grab a bite."

I gave her my basin number, thanked Mariana for the tea, and wished her well.

I put the top down on the convertible and my doggie greeted me as though I'd been gone a week and not an hour. He sat attentively and listened as I reviewed the little I learned. "Her eyes had sunk so deep into their sockets, that I doubt if I would recognize her on the street. Dick's wife looks the same as the walking dead. I tell ya, Siggie, by comparison, Butch looked better."

"Woof."

"No, I am not kidding. The woman looks like overcooked crap. Anyway, she has no love for Butch. Said he got everything he deserved."

"Woof."

"Hey, guess what? I found out they own a big cabin cruiser moored in our marina. I've never seen Dick Green wearing anything except a black wool suit, rep tie, and wingtips. Bet he doesn't own a pair of jeans or deck shoes." I giggled. "Do you think he wears a three-piece suit on his boat? The same way Richard Nixon walked on the beach in a suit." Siggie stared at me blankly. "Sorry, I forgot. He was way before your time. Nixon was President of the country in the seventies. A few times when he came to California and walked on the beach, he wore a business suit."

Siggie's ears perked up at the mention of the beach. "WOOF."

I ignored his not-so-subtle-hint. "Anyway, Dick's wife needs money badly and is selling the boat way under market value for a fast sale."

"Woof."

"No kidding. I tried to talk her out of it, but her mind is made up. Boy, does she hate Butch with a capital H-ate." I slid my eyes over to Siggie. "She looks awful, but we shouldn't write her off the suspect list. She works out at a gym and kept a prescription for valium in the medicine chest. She blames Butch for what happened to Dick. She is convinced Butch set Dick up. I'm not sure about the means, but she sure has one heck of a motive. I'm gonna run all this past Snip. If she agrees, I'm gonna call Detective Jones."

"Woof."

"Good. Glad you agree. Wanna go to the park?"

"WOOF! WOOF!"

"Ok, ok. Hold your horses. I can't go any faster."

"Woof."

"No, I can't."

"Woof, woof, woof."

"You do so know why not. Because a motorcycle cop hides behind the Bonds Brothers supermarket on Lincoln at the Marina Freeway. My car insurance is already sky-high. The last thing we need is a speeding ticket to jack up my rate even higher."

****

After a quick romp with my hound at the doggie park to assuage my guilt for leaving him locked in the car while I questioned Mariana, I dropped Siggie off at the boat for a play date with my dock mate, Muriel Lobowsky. I drove downtown to Mermaid, and headed for Queenie's office. I picked up Queenie's phone and called my favorite ME. "Snip, it's me. I just got back from Dick and Mariana Green's house." I whistled. "Man, does she hate Butch. A bottle of valium is in her medicine chest. She has a World-Wide Gym membership, so maybe she uses muscle relaxers too."

Doctor Death laughed out loud. "Sorry to disappoint you Nancy Drew but valium wasn't found in the victim's system. The good news for your friend Ms. Levine is neither was Celebro. I wouldn't get too excited about Mariana Green's gym membership. All it means is she's health conscious. It doesn't prove a thing. So, don't run

59

to point the finger at Mrs. Green yet. Hey, I've gotta split. I've three new patients waiting." Before I could respond with one of my many snappy retorts, the line went dead.

Queenie said without a trace of irony. "Sounds as if Mariana Green is a dead-end." I grinned like a loon. She narrowed her eyes. "Why are you so happy?"

"Lab tests indicated no Celebro in Butch's system."

Queenie yelped for joy, then came back down to Earth. "I'll bet Jones still has me in his sights."

I said, "Hopefully, our condolence call to Kelly will be more useful. I'm leaving the office early to feed and walk Siggie. I'll meet you at Diane's house at six tonight."

Queenie asked, "What time are you leaving?"

"I'm in production meetings until around four. I'm leaving right after the last one ends. Why?"

Queenie said, "My design meeting with Gary ends around then. I'll leave at the same time and follow you to the marina. We can grab a bite before our appointment and go in one car."

I said, "Works for me. We have to eat anyway, so why not together?"

"Then it's a date. See you later."

****

Queenie and I walked out of the factory together to the employee parking lot past the warehouse loading docks. She parked two spaces before mine. I put the top down and slid into the well-worn driver's seat. I turned the ignition key, but instead of the two-eighty-nine roaring to life, a series of clicks and then nothing. Huh? The battery isn't more than three months old.

Queenie pulled up behind me and rolled down her

window. "You waiting for me?"

I shook my head. "Nope, the car won't start. I don't get it. The battery is practically brand new." I held up my cell phone. "Hopefully the auto club won't take all night."

Queenie said, "Thank God it's not raining or you'd be waiting forever. Do you want to meet me at Coast Burgers? The place is always jammed. Better for one of us to get there fast and grab a table."

I dipped my head. "If you don't mind, I'd rather you wait and make sure the auto club shows up and if they do, they jump the battery ok. Even if they arrive quickly, we'll never get back to the beach, see about my pooch, eat, and get to Diane's on time. I better call Muriel and see if she will take care of Siggie. We can eat at a place close to Diane's."

****

The auto club guy wiped his greasy hands on his stained uniform pants leg before he opened the hood. He poked around the engine and whistled through his teeth.

I said, "The battery is only a few months old. It must be defective."

The guy shook his head and waved me to stand next to him. "Nothing is wrong with your battery."

I looked at him kind of wonky. "So, why doesn't the car start?"

He pointed to the front of the engine. "You've got a much bigger problem. You're missing a spark plug. You're not going anyplace without it."

Queenie and I followed the tow truck to my mechanic Johnny's station. Johnny told me to come back around nine o'clock to pick up the car.

Chapter Nine

Kelly poured the coffee and passed the unmatching cups around. I counted my blessings. We might not learn anything useful, but at least we two coffee hounds dodged another session with bitter tea. Kelly, Diane, Queenie, and I sat around Diane's old-fashioned Formica kitchen table chatting and sipping like four old friends catching up on one another's lives. The difference between Kelly and Diane? Startling is an understatement. With red-rimmed eyes and a defeated expression on her tired face, gorgeous Kelly Oldham shared the same rundown look of a badly maintained car.

By comparison, a relaxed Diane was seemingly carefree. Diane and Butch were colleagues and old friends long before either of them met Kelly. With her friend viciously murdered, you'd think she'd be a little more upset. Seems weird. I chided myself. I am a fine one to talk. Considering my crazy reaction to a death, I am hardly in a position to judge the way someone else deals with it. Diane might be one of those stoic types trying to put up a brave front and be strong for Kelly's sake. Or, maybe she hated Butch more than Kelly. The answer to that question might also reveal who murdered Butch Oldham.

I turned to Kelly. "Are you selling the house? I imagine you'd hardly want to stay living in it."

Kelly pursed her lips. "It's not mine to sell. Butch

and I signed a prenup. Above and beyond the terms of the prenup, Butch left his entire estate to his children."

Diane spat the words out like a piece of rotten fruit. "She's got her clothes, the car, a few baubles of jewelry, and the money from the prenup. We're done."

Queenie said, "You were getting a divorce, right?"

Kelly nodded yes.

I asked, "When I ran into you the day of the murder, you said you came to the factory to work out the divorce terms with Butch. So, did you finalize the terms?"

Kelly's laugh turned as bitter as Mariana's tea. "No such luck. Somebody fileted him before we had a chance to work out the terms of the agreement."

Diane narrowed her eyes. "Why all the questions?"

Kelly squirmed in her seat when Queenie said, "It's no secret the spouse is always the first one the cops suspect." Queenie smiled at Kelly. "Guess Butch was worth more to you alive than dead."

Kelly opened her mouth to reply but clamped it shut when Diane responded for her. "You can't negotiate with a corpse." Diane lifted the carafe and offered more coffee. As she filled my cup, I pointed to the bandage covering her left hand. "Pretty nasty injury."

Diane put the carafe back on the trivet and glanced at her bandaged hand as though she just discovered it. "Oh, this? It's nothing. Looks a lot worse than it is. I cut myself while changing the oil in my truck."

Girlie-girl Queenie wiggled her fingers and laughed. "You'd never catch me fiddling under the hood of a car. And risk ruining my manicure? Not a chance."

I said, "Other than turning the ignition on and off, the only mechanical thing I am capable of is changing a flat tire. My dad insisted all us kids learn. I started my apparel career as a road rep in the deep southern states. Good thing Dad insisted I learn to change a tire. I had a couple of flats in the middle of no place." I laughed at the memory. "If I didn't change it myself, I'd still be waiting for a tow truck to arrive."

Diane took a large glass from the middle shelf of a glazed knotty pine cabinet. She went to the sink, opened the tap, and drank two full glasses of water. She put the glass in the sink and turned to face the three of us seated at the table. "I come from a family of mechanics, so, it's something I've been around all my life."

Queenie pointed to Diane's left hand. "I bet the injury put a crimp in your golf game."

A scrolled tattoo of the letters *TT* bulged as Diane flexed the biceps on her left arm. The letters **SF** were tattooed on the right forearm below the elbow. "You're right. No problem driving, but putting and chipping won't be pretty."

Queenie asked, "I've seen you playing out at Ranchito Park. You're pretty good on the links. Who taught you to play?"

Diane said, "My dad and older brothers all golf. I started as their caddy. When I was old enough, Dad took me out alone and taught me. What about you?"

Queenie said, "My dad also taught me to play." She grinned. "While I was a duffer, we played every week. But since I've started beating him, he's threatened not to play with me anymore."

Queenie was being uncharacteristically modest. She is actually a scratch golfer, and has even hit a couple of holes in one. She is so good; most men think twice before entering the swimwear industry charity tournaments if her name is on the player's roster. I walked the course with her a few times and became interested in learning to play. Queenie started giving me lessons. The prior weekend, Queenie and I bumped into Diane at the 19th Hole, the restaurant at the Ranchito Park Golf Course. Queenie plays in a standing foursome there with three female industry competitors Sunday mornings. Diane took an imaginary swing with her left arm towards me. "So, are the lessons going well so far?"

I sighed. "Queenie has done her best, but having a right-handed teacher for a leftie has been a challenge. We tried making me into a rightie, but I have no power in my right arm. I can't swing the club hard enough to hit the ball more than a few yards. We switched me back to a leftie, but it's confusing for us both with her instructing me backward."

Diane took another imaginary swing with her left arm. "I'm a southpaw too. You own your own clubs or do you rent them?"

I said, "Rent by the session for now. If I get past the lesson stage to playing a full round, I would consider buying clubs, even though a special order takes forever to fill." I laughed. "The pro at the club shop called around. Not too many courses kept left-handed junior-size women's golf clubs in stock."

Diane drank two more glasses of water and said, "Stand up." I stood, and she gave me the once-over. "I'm only four or five inches taller than you. My clubs would probably do you just fine. I'm not a scratch golfer, but I'm still pretty good. I bet with some practice and a little spit and polish; you'll be playing almost as good as a seasoned player in no time at all. No charge for the lessons or use of the clubs. Buy me lunch and a couple of brewskies at the 19th Hole after the lessons and we will be square."

I rubbed my hands together and grinned "Fantastic. Let me know the next time you're playing, and I'll come along."

Diane's ranch-style house was in the older part of the Cheviot Hills section of West Los Angeles. The wing-style floor plan was a classic 1950's craftsman with two small bedrooms but only one bathroom. The rectangular living room was the center of the house. A narrow kitchen, service porch, and a small den were on the left side, and the two bedrooms with the one bathroom between them on the right side.

I downed the third cup of coffee, asked for directions to the john, and excused myself. The floor plan provided some distance between the bathroom and the kitchen. I couldn't dawdle too long, but at least no one heard me going through the medicine chest and bathroom drawers. You can only flush the toilet so many times before someone checks to see if you're sick. A vial of Diabinese prescribed for Diane sat on the top shelf of the medicine cabinet. I made a mental note to ask Snip the type of medication it is. I flushed the toilet again for good measure.

On the way back to the kitchen, I glanced into the master bedroom. Hopeless nosy parker me couldn't resist the open closet door. I shouldn't have, but I sneaked a peek. Kelly's frilly girlie clothes hung on the left side, and Diane's masculine wardrobe was on the right. The question of where Butch's widow now lived has been answered. I thumbed my way through Kelly's wardrobe looking for who knows…? Regrettably, for my trouble, I found only a few quarters in the front pocket of a pair of pricey designer jeans.

Good thing I'd just been to the bathroom or I'd peed myself when Diane tapped me on the shoulder. "So, are you just naturally nosy, or are you looking for something in particular?" She narrowed her eyes. "You're a little too short to borrow her clothes."

I dropped the edge of the sexy black lace floor-length negligee fast as a red-hot poker and flashed a shit-eating grin. "Just admiring a wardrobe I'll never be able to wear. It's gorgeous, but you're right. I'm way too short for a full-length negligee." I twittered a nervous laugh. "Besides, I live on a drafty houseboat. Fuzzy fleece jammies are more my speed." I held my breath. Would she buy my cock and bull story? Miss Marple must have been looking out for me. Diane shrugged and we went back to the kitchen. I whistled past the cemetery for once.

The four of us made small talk for fifteen more minutes, then I gave Queenie the high sign. I needed to get to Johnny's before he closed and had to tell Queenie about the medicine chest. Queenie has lots of doctors and pharmacists in her family. Maybe she's familiar with Diabinese.

Halfway to the car, Queenie asked, "Anything interesting in the john?"

I nodded. "Something called Diabinese was prescribed for Diane, but I'm not familiar with it. Maybe it's a muscle relaxant. Are you?" Queenie shook her head no.

I said, "Ok, I'll call Snip and find out." I grinned. "You'll be happy to hear even though Butch's house isn't hers, Kelly isn't homeless. Her clothes are hanging in the same closet as Diane's. Maybe the rumors of Kelly dumping Butch for Diane are true. "

Queenie wrinkled her nose. "Kelly looked awful. Either she killed Butch and is sorry or she's really upset he was murdered."

I said, "No clue as to which one, but as bad as Kelly looks, Diane certainly hasn't lost any sleep over Butch."

Queenie shrugged. "Maybe she just put on a brave face for Kelly's sake. Are you going to take Diane up on her golf lesson offer?"

I took an imaginary swing. "Absolutely. It's a win-win. I learn to play correctly for a leftie and maybe we get lucky. In a relaxed setting, she might let her guard down and I get some valuable information out of her. Diane might hate Butch with a purple passion for the rotten way he supposedly treated Kelly, but even so, she looks way too ok with his murder. Begs the question why."

Queenie grinned. "The lessons might be free, but if she drinks the way she did at last year's Christmas party, you're going to go broke with her bar tab at the 19th Hole."

We walked past Kelly's sportscar and I laughed at her vanity license plate. X Shiksa. A Shiksa was a derogatory name Jews give to gentile women. Did Kelly convert to Judaism for Butch? Nah. Kelly Oldham married for money, not love. She took the easier conversion route by becoming Jewish by injection, so to speak.

Queenie parked in the driveway behind Diane's truck. The light from the streetlamp hit Diane's vanity license plate, 2 TEAMS, at an odd angle and caught my eye. Being an LA commuter means spending a lot of time in bumper-to-bumper freeway traffic. I amused myself trying to figure out the meanings of the vanity license plates. When Diane worked at Mermaid, she parked in the space next to mine. I never figured out the meaning of Diane's license plate. I always intended to ask her but never got around to it. I made a mental note to ask her about it on the day we play golf.

I turned and pointed back to the house. "This turned out to be a big nothing burger. The only thing we learned is they are both coffee drinkers and take their java with cream but no sugar." I opened the car door. "Time to move on. Once I pick up my car, I'm going back to Mermaid to get into the employee files in Human Resources. The factory will be empty by then. A list of medications people take might be on their employee profiles. Craziest things have happened than this…maybe we'll get lucky, and someone is taking a muscle relaxant and it'll be in their profile. It's a long shot, but I'm running out of ideas and we're running out of time."

****

As we drove east on Olympic, Queenie asked, "How exactly do you lose a spark plug?" She smirked. "Check your purse. Your hobo is big enough to carry a compact car. Maybe the spark plug is in your bag."

I stuck my tongue out at her. "Aren't you the funny one? You should consider taking your act out on the road."

Queenie dropped me off at Johnny's and headed back to the beach. The convertible sat in a bay with the hood up. Johnny motioned for me to lean over and look at the front of the engine. "You see the cylinder head at the top of the engine?"

I crossed my eyes. He might as well be speaking in tongues. "Surely you jest. I couldn't tell the difference between a cylinder head from a head of lettuce."

He smirked. "With all the times your car is in the shop, you should be a master mechanic by now." He grinned as I gave him the middle finger salute. He pointed to the top of the engine. "See the wire hanging loose? It should be connected to a spark plug, but it's missing from the pocket under the cylinder head. Somebody yanked the spark plug out and tore off the wire lead that connects to the spark plug. You could crank your baby until the cows come home, but without a spark plug, you weren't going anyplace."

I narrowed my eyes. "You're saying the spark plug didn't get loose from the engine vibrations and fall out?"

Johnny shook his head. "Nosiree. I'm saying somebody tampered with your car." Regrettably, this isn't the first time my eagle-eyed mechanic found something suspicious under the hood of my convertible. Johnny narrowed his eyes. "You either pissed somebody off or somebody is sending you a message."

Somebody knew I often worked late. And if I worked late enough, I'd probably be the only one in the building. Our factory isn't in the hood, but you certainly wouldn't call the neighborhood ritzy. Our offices are adjacent to the produce mart, an area busy from 2:00 AM to 2:00 PM. If I worked alone in the evening hours, the area is a virtual ghost town. Someone wanted me stranded and alone in a not-so-safe part of town once the sun goes down. Yikes.

Chapter Ten

The Mermaid executive offices were dark as the bottom of a witch's cauldron as I unlocked the front door and shut off the alarm. An involuntary shiver settled into my chest and squeezed my heart as I reset the alarm. Not wanting to draw any unwanted attention to a lit building from the street, I turned on the one interior hall light and cautiously made my way down the main hall to the executive aisle. The hall light shone brightly like a lighthouse beacon. Or maybe it was just my nerves battling my resolve. Toss a coin.

I checked my watch. Eight on the nose. I'd worked late often enough to remember the cleaning crew finished an hour ago. Thank goodness. One less thing to worry about. Nonetheless, I surveyed the length of the hallway for unexpected visitors and gave it the all-clear. Mine was the only car in the parking lot and the building was locked and dark, but to be on the safe side, I killed the hall light.

I pulled a flashlight out of the hobo and beamed it around. Of course, if I'd shined the light on someone lurking around the building, imagine that confrontation? Somehow "good evening, nice to see you" didn't sound quite right. Merde. Too late to turn back, so I squared my shoulders and made my way to HR and hoped for the best.

No matter which way I turned it, the door handle to

the Human Resources office wouldn't budge. I foraged through the hobo bag for a tool to jimmy the lock. Don't overthink this, I told myself. Maybe something simple, like my office key? As if. I should only be so lucky. It fit in the keyhole, but the lock didn't disengage. So much for a simple solution.

I better get creative or it would be time to boogie. Which right at the moment, didn't seem too bad an idea. I shook it off and focused. They say God helps those who help themselves. Car key? Long enough, but past the teeth, it was too thick to fit completely into the keyhole. Paper clip? Not even close. Ballpoint pen tip? It fit, but not long enough. HR director Eleanor Conklin's files might hold the answers to my questions, but there'd be no getting to them without a key. Her office was locked tighter than a drum. I might as well burgle Fort Knox.

Just when I was ready to throw in the towel and call it quits, the burglary Goddess smiled down on me. I pulled a manicure set with a metal nail file in it out of the side pocket of the hobo. I stuck the tip in. Fantastic! A perfect fit. But would it do the trick? My heart thumped in my throat and I held my breath. Two counter clockwise turns and bingo, bongo, jackpot. I twisted the handle and pushed the door open. Hotdiggidy. Way to go. Now you're cookin', Nancy Drew.

I closed the door behind me and relocked it. Better safe than sorry. I turned on the light and put the hobo down on Eleanor's metal desk. On the other side of the door, creak, creak, creak. My heart almost exploded out of my chest. Considering Johnny's warning, anyone with a brain ditches this crazy idea and heads straight for the barn. But no one ever confused me with Albert Einstein. I strained my ears. Creak, creak, creak. What was it?

Unless the building was settling as some older buildings do, the better question is *who* is it? Who was I expecting? The boogeyman or Butch Oldham's ghost? Was it the emptiness of the building giving me the industrial-strength heebie-jeebies? Or me walking on Butch Oldham's grave? Since he'd been murdered only a few thousand yards away, that might be it. Or, maybe I was just scared of the dark? Then the noise stopped as suddenly as it started. I shook it off and pushed those spooky thoughts aside to focus on the job at hand.

The employee files held a treasure trove of information. David Workman has Epstein-Barr. I wracked my brain. Epstein-Barr, Epstein-Barr? I'd heard of this condition from someplace. Come on, come on. Think of where you heard it, or it'll drive you nuts. Oh, yeah. I mentally snapped my fingers. David has the same condition as my mother's canasta friend Carol. Oh boy. Mom derisively called it the faker's disease. Doctors often diagnosed it as a chronic hypochondriac. I filed the interesting tidbit of information in my memory for future use, but the pill of disappointment was bitter to swallow. The strongest medication listed in David's file is valium. Big whoop. This is LA. Even Queenie's cleaning lady sees a shrink twice a week and takes valium. Guess dusting and mopping floors are a lot more stressful than one would ever imagine.

I paged through the next file and a stab of sympathy nicked my heart. Tireless Mermaid head patternmaker Bernice Price has arthritic wrists and takes Tylenol extra strength twice a day.

Head designer Gary Burkett takes Dyanavel XR, an Amphetamine prescribed for ADHD. It certainly explains why the talented head designer bounces off the walls so much of the time.

I closed the last employee file with the weight of defeat crushing my hopes to help Queenie. Interesting information and insights into co-workers' behavior, but nothing incriminating. I exhausted all my ideas. I took the car keys out of the hobo. No point sticking around. The keys slipped out of my hand and bounced. Cripes. I crawled on my hands and knees and stopped a few times to wave the flashlight around. Good thing, or otherwise, the keys would be lost forever. It is beyond me how, but they landed behind the file cabinet I'd missed in the back corner concealed by a sad-looking artificial plant.

I put the keys back in the hobo and went through the files. The top two drawers were a big bust. Nothing but company employee manuals and blank employment applications. Same with the middle drawer filled to the brim with state and federal employee regulation guides. If the last drawer proved equally worthless, then it was time to throw in the towel and boogie. My knees cracked as I crouched down on my haunches to open the bottom drawer.

The ex-employee files were organized by date of an employment separation, rather than alphabetically, with the most recent separation dates at the front of the drawer. I'd no sooner opened Diane Gentry's exit file when noise in the hall diverted my attention. I killed the light, shoved the file drawer closed with my foot, and cringed as the drawer squeaked loud as a trapped mouse.

I crept to the door and put my ear against it. Footsteps and the uneven gait of a big person wearing heavy boots clomped across the hall. The noise in the hall grew louder. Not a good sign. I desperately looked around for a place to hide. I shoved Eleanor's chair out of the way and dove under the desk ass first facing back towards the far wall. I leaned back and yelped in surprise as I fell backward onto the carpet. Eleanor's desk opened in the front. Either the company bought her a cheaper desk or Eleanor preferred to stretch out her legs. I sat up too quickly and banged my head on the edge of the metal desk opening as I tried to slide back through. I angled to the side to pull myself out. I misjudged the width of the back desk opening. I dropped the hobo upside down and naturally, everything spilled out all over the floor. I threw all the crap back in without looking and zipped the bag closed. Would I ever find my car keys? Doubtful. I sucked as a second-story woman.

The noise grew closer. If I got caught, I'd be fired for sure. Since I often work late, the explanation of being in the building is easy *if* I'd been in my office. All the executives are given keys to the building and the alarm combination. But a plausible explanation for breaking into Eleanor's office and poking around in her files? Not a one. My ample BS skills deserted me. The footsteps stopped in front of Eleanor's office. The handle of the door jiggled. Thank God I'd locked the door from the inside.

I bought myself a few precious seconds to think. Other than under the desk, where to hide? Behind the file cabinets? I shook off the idea. Not enough room behind them, and they were too heavy to move. Behind the sad artificial plant? Not big enough. Even if it was, the dust would give me away if it made me sneeze. Just in the nick of time, the burglary Goddess came through again. I spied a small storage closet across the room cattycorner from the desk. I guesstimated the distance and prayed Eleanor kept the closet unlocked. If not, count me

75

professionally screwed.

A key slipped into the keyhole and the lock tumblers of Eleanor's office door disengaged. With no more than a count of three Mississippi's before the office door opened, it was now or never. I grabbed the hobo and Diane's file and ran for the closet. Thank God the narrow closet door opened. Just as I squeezed into the closet and closed myself in, Eleanor's office door opened. I plastered myself to the back of the closet. A thin line of light shined under the storage door. Alberto the night guard muttered to himself as he looked around. How did I forget about him?

I almost hurled as the closet door handle jiggled. I slipped off my shoes and put them into the back corner of the floor. I shoved the office supplies to the left and climbed up the narrow shelving. I wedged into the right corner and hung onto the edge of the shelf with my fingertips. My hands slicked with sweat. The shelf slipped from my grasp. I bit my lip hard enough to draw blood as the right corner of the shelf pinched my ass. I shifted to the left and the flimsy shelf jiggled. I prayed it would hold my weight and the guard didn't look too high up. The closet door opened a crack and I drew back as far as possible. I held my breath, shut my eyes, and prayed my career wasn't about to go up in flames. I cracked open an eye. The closet door clicked closed. For some reason, Alberto changed his mind. If I could restart my heart, I'd be in great shape.

The thin sliver of light under the closet door went dark. Alberto's heavy footfalls were music to my ears as he walked out of Eleanor's office and closed the door. I let out my breath only after the door lock tumblers clicked into the locked position.

I stayed in the closet for another ten minutes in case Alberto returned. I faced the back of the closet and turned on the flashlight. I held it up to Diane's open file and scanned her medical records. Holy guacamole! Diane *was* diabetic and took insulin twice a day. This might be the break we needed. I started to call Queenie but stopped mid-dial. My luck, Alberto has the ears of a bat.

I cautiously opened the closet door and listened. No footfalls, but Alberto might be in the next office for all I knew. I debated whether to chance it and go through the rest of the files in the bottom drawer. I blew off the idea. The files were in order of most recent departure, so whoever else's file is in the bottom drawer was probably long gone from the company before Butch died. The smart money said time to get out of Dodge while the getting is good. I slipped my shoes back on, counted my blessings, and crept out of the closet.

I fired up Eleanor's copier. I paced with the impatience of an expectant father while the machine took forever and a day to warm up. Two seconds away from just stealing the file and damned the consequences, the green light finally blinked on. I copied Diane's file and put the originals back in the drawer. I stuffed the copies in the hobo, gave a cursory look around Eleanor's office to make sure I left it as I found it, and got the hell out before my luck ran out.

I prayed Alberto finished his factory rounds and had moved on to the warehouse by now. But since I was unsure of his location, I couldn't take the chance of turning on the hall light. I crawled along at a snail's pace, plastered to the walls waving the flashlight low on the carpeted floor until I got back to the lobby. I disarmed and reset the alarm, locked the building, ran-walked around the corner to the back parking lot, and dove into the convertible.

Chapter Eleven

I called Queenie as I drove away from the scene of the crime. "I think I found something. Diane Gentry is diabetic and takes insulin every day. It means Kelly has access to syringes."

Queenie's war-whoop probably awakened the dead. "Holy crap! That's fantastic!"

I muttered more to myself than to Queenie, "Why didn't she keep the syringes in the bathroom?"

Queenie logically surmised, "Insulin is refrigerated. Maybe she keeps the syringes in the kitchen."

I said, "You're right. I'm on my way back to the marina. I'll meet you at your house. We should call Snip and ask about Diabinese. Diane does a lot of physical things. Maybe it's a muscle relaxant."

****

The clock on Queenie's kitchen wall said unless it was an emergency, it was way past a decent time to call. Sophie Cutler got up insanely early to jog before going to work. No doubt she was asleep. Was this an emergency? No way to tell yet, but from the cheap seats, this wouldn't keep until morning. Besides, Queenie would burst a gut by then. I cringed at the sound of Sophie's voice thick with sleep. "Snip, it's me, Holly. Listen, I'm sorry to bother you so late at night but this just can't wait. What medical condition is Diabinese prescribed for?"

I pictured her sitting up from her futon and checking the clock. "Uh, yeah. Lemme think." I winced as she made a jaw-cracking loud yawn. "It's prescribed for diabetics." In a nanosecond, her synapses fired and she snapped wide awake. "Why? Are you ok?"

Such a pal. Snip wasn't angry about being woken late at night, she just worried about me. "No worries. I'm fine. We paid a condolence call to Kelly Oldham. We met her over at Diane Gentry's house in West LA. I went into the bathroom and found a bottle of Diabinese prescribed to Diane." I crossed my fingers behind my back and lied like a rug. "Queenie told me Diane is diabetic and takes insulin daily. So, it means Kelly has access to syringes."

She mused. "Hmm. That's interesting."

It was downright weird of Sophie not to ask how Queenie knew Diane is diabetic. Normally, Snip's mind was as sharp as a steel trap. No way she'd miss asking an obvious question. Guess being awakened out of a dead sleep took her a little off her game. Amusement tickled her voice. "So, Nancy Drew, find any syringes while snooping around?"

I laughed. "No, but I couldn't exactly search the whole house."

Doctor Death sniped, "Gee, Nancy, I'm kinda disappointed in you."

I laughed. "No way to make you happy."

Then Snip said, "Come to think of it, you wouldn't find any syringes. Diabinese is taken orally, not by syringe."

Talk about a mood killer. Our fleeting moment of victory deflated faster than a pinpricked balloon. I moaned my disappointment. "Crap."

Snip tsked. "Don't be so hard on yourself. You had no way to know."

I said, "Do me a favor. Pass this information along to Detective Jones. It's still important."

Sophie cackled like a laying hen. "I don't see any way to do it without cutting my own throat, but I'll try. Good night kiddo." I disconnected the call and Queenie looked at me cross-eyed as I gave her a high-five. "We've been looking in the right church but the wrong pew. We stumbled onto the real killer. It's Diane. Not Kelly."

Queenie rolled her eyes and snorted a laugh. "I wish."

Despite her surprisingly generous offer to give me golf lessons, neither Queenie nor I particularly cared for Diane. She was a bully at the office for no other reason than she had the power of Butch Oldham behind her. And Diane constantly threw her weight around. We were both happier than two pigs rolling in the mud the day Diane suddenly and inexplicably, resigned.

Queenie waved her dismissal. "I dunno. This just doesn't pass the sniff test. If Diane takes insulin orally and not with a syringe, the cop's gonna say so who cares if she's diabetic. And I'd agree with him. Given the timing between Butch getting laid and getting killed, it's reasonable to assume the person Butch screwed is also the killer. Since Diane is a lesbian, she's a poor candidate. My money is still on Kelly. She still has the most to lose."

I shrugged. "Then you better discount Kelly too. We've all heard the rumor Kelly left Butch for Diane." I shrugged. "Kelly's clothes hung next to Diane's in the master bedroom closet, not in the spare room. It looks like the rumor is true."

Queenie grinned devilishly. "Even if it's true, Kelly had *millions* of reasons to bang Butch till he got saddle sore for a month." She waggled her brows. "And a whole lot of motivation to play for the home team one more time."

I sighed. "You're probably right. Kelly makes more sense any way you look at it." As I said it, I shook my head with frustration. "I keep circling back to Diane for some reason and I've no idea exactly why. Something important about Diane is niggling at the back of my brain, but I can't bring it to the front. It's driving me nuts."

I glanced at the wall clock and grabbed the hobo. It was way past my bedtime and I was bone tired. Almost getting caught burgling Eleanor's office wiped me out. Muriel fed and walked Siggie, so he'd be raring to play. Fabulous. All I wanted to do? Stop thinking and get horizontal. I said, "It's been a long day. Maybe it'll come to me tomorrow." I waved her not to see me out. "Hang tight, kiddo. We're close to figuring this out. I feel it in my bones." I said with as much conviction as I could muster.

****

The next morning Queenie and I left the Rampart police station holding our twin threatening letters madder than a pair of wet hens. After receiving the same unsigned letter in our office mailboxes, we made an appointment with Detective Jones. The notes were written with letters cut out of magazines and said: "*Quit asking questions or you're next.*" Jones displayed zero interest in having the crudely written notes tested for fingerprints to determine the author. His only comment?

"You don't want threatening letters? Take the author's advice. Do us both a favor and quit interfering in my investigation. Stop asking questions and let me do my job."

We stomped out of Jones' office and Queenie waved the threatening letter towards Miguel's office at the end of the hallway. "Maybe your boyfriend will pay more attention to this than his detective?"

I shook my head no. "Why bother? I need another lecture like I need a migraine. Besides, don't you remember? Miguel made the same speech after we received one of these types of threatening letters while he investigated the Bunny Frank murder."

We got back to the factory after wasting our time at the Rampart precinct no safer nor closer to revealing the author. I focused on unfinished projects to calm down. As I left our head patternmaker Bernice Price's office, David bellowed over the intercom, "Holly Schlivnik, 211. Holly, extension 211." The patternmaking area is closer to David's office than to mine, so rather than take the time to get to a phone to answer his page, I went down the hall to see what his royal highness needed.

David has an open-door policy. If his door is open, no knock is necessary, just go in. Two steps from my crossing the threshold of his office, Detective Jones's baritone voice came over David's speakerphone. I backpedaled faster than a circus clown on a unicycle. I plastered myself to the wall adjacent to David's door and eavesdropped on the call.

The cop's angry voice boomed over the speaker. "Mr. Workman, I'm sorry, I just flat out don't believe you. You lied to me the last time and you're lying again. You most certainly did blackmail Mr. Oldham."

David sniffed with righteous indignation. "I most certainly did not. And I resent your insinuation."

Jones cleared his throat. "Cut the crap, Mr. Workman. I've spoken to Ms. Gentry since the last time you and I spoke. You were aware Ms. Gentry and Mr. Oldham's wife are lovers. It's the way you forced Ms. Gentry to resign. You threatened to tell Mr. Oldham about their dirty little secret if Ms. Gentry defied you."

Jones laughed as David sputtered his denial. "Then you turned the tables on all of them. You confronted Mr. Oldham with the truth."

Oh boy. David Workman is not a man used to being called out by anyone, especially by some pushy cop. "You're dead wrong detective." David twittered a nervous laugh. "Even if I told him, the great Butch Oldham was way too egotistical to believe me."

Jones snarled. "Whether he believed you or not is beside the point, sir. He couldn't take a chance you didn't make it up, and let it get out in the industry Butch Oldham's wife left him for another woman. So, he paid for your silence."

David clucked his tongue. "Well, then I'm the one who should be dead not Butch, don't you think?"

Jones mused. "Maybe you and the victim's wife worked together and got rid of your mutual problem."

David snorted his derisive reply to such a tall tale. "If I blackmailed Butch, why would I kill the goose laying the golden egg?"

Jones shot back, "Either way it's a win-win for you. Alive Oldham pays through the nose for your silence. Dead Oldham relinquished the keys to the castle back to the prince." Jones laughed. "Last time, you said for you it's all about the money. Maybe Oldham's wife is so happy you killed him she pays you a king's ransom to say thanks."

David laughed out loud. "Detective, I don't know what you've been smoking but I want some. Give me a ring if you get any actual evidence to back up your fairy tale. Until then, don't waste my time." And then David Workman slammed down the phone. Holy guacamole.

I counted three Mississippi's and walked into David's office. "You bellowed, my master?"

Chapter Twelve

I nodded good evening to the slant-winged old crane living on my dock and turned the Adirondack chair to face the fiery orange sun. I already fed, walked, and played with my pooch. Now it was my time to relax. I cranked up the stereo and took my first restorative sip of Chardonnay. Then the cell phone rang. Crap. The stinker of a day was a doozy of a bad combination. Long and challenging. Who does a girl need to bribe to buy a few minutes of peace? Area code 225? Where the Sam Hill is that? I glanced at my watch and debated whether or not to answer. This time of night, no doubt a telemarketer. Screw 'em. I let it ring and sipped more wine. Remarkably, the damned phone kept ringing. I pushed the on button and barked, "Whatever you're selling I'm sure I don't need it. So, make it short and sweet."

My heart lurched at the familiar deep throaty laugh. "Hello. Is this Holly Swimsuit?" Even after all those years, his soft southern drawl still thrilled me beyond words or good sense. This was no telemarketer peddling solar panels. This was a ghost from my past tap-dancing his way across my heart again. The one I'd safely tucked away into the deepest recesses of my memory. The one I'd buried in the back of my heart to avoid spending the rest of my life second-guessing myself till I drove myself mad. From the pounding of my heart at the sound of his voice, the memory wasn't tucked away nearly deep enough. My wise nana always said since it is the one you can do nothing about, regret is the worst human emotion. Everybody has one. Buddy LaValle was mine.

He tagged me with the nickname Holly Swimsuit, and it stuck with me throughout my career. We were colleagues and fellow road reps traveling together in the deep southern states. Then it all changed after I complicated everything by falling in love with him. Just as I'd worked up the nerve to tell him, he broke my heart by introducing me to his fiancée. I moved back to LA without ever telling him my true feelings. Buddy LaValle was the one I'd let slip away.

As though he was an echo calling from someplace back in our history, his smoky voice crooned deep and low. "Holly, this is Buddy…. Don't you remember me? Buddy LaValle from the other LA?"

It was our standing joke. We both hailed from LA. Me from Los Angeles and he from Louisiana.

"Hello?" Buddy said, breaking into the reverie back in time. "Guess I dialed the wrong number. Sorry to bother you."

I snapped out of my mental game of ping pong seconds before he disconnected. "Wait! Yes, it's me. Holly Swimsuit." I glugged a ginormous gulp of liquid courage. And then someone whose voice sounded remarkably the same as mine said, "Of course, I remember you, Buddy. It's good to hear your voice too. It's been a long time."

****

LAPD Captain Miguel Martinez and I sat across from one another in a red leather booth large enough to seat a basketball team in the Blue China Moon Café two blocks east of the California Apparel Mart. At six-foot-two and all toned muscle, with broad shoulders, a narrow waist, and slim hips, dark-haired and mustachioed Miguel stood out in a crowded room.

The handsome cop and I shared a stormy history. Homicide Detective Miguel Martinez was in charge of the case when I discovered buying office big shot Bunny Frank's corpse in the mart parking elevator trussed up with shipping tape as tight as a mummy and a Gotham Swimwear bikini stuffed in her mouth.

The detective and I had a rollercoaster-worthy bumpy relationship. For some inexplicable reason, he didn't cotton to my interfering with his investigation or telling him how to do his job. I solved the case and captured the killer, yet the ungrateful detective still didn't do cartwheels. Go figure. Two murders later, the detective was promoted to Lieutenant, and then in record breaking time, he moved up to Captain. Coincidence? Not on your life. By solving the high-profile Frank case and handing the killer to Martinez on a platter, I increased his case closure rate substantially and moved him up the corporate ladder at a breakneck pace.

Miguel and the detective on a different case visited me in the hospital while I recovered from injuries sustained at the hand of another killer. Undeniable sparks ignited as our fingers grazed one another's when Miguel handed me a bouquet of daisies. We took it slow and easy and started to date. We test drove the relationship with occasional lunches at the Blue China Moon to see if it went anyplace. As we found common interests in convertible cars and music-jazz for him and oldies rock and roll for me- the relationship grew from lunch companions to a work in progress. We've been dating for some time now. We're not exclusive to one another, but neither of us dated anyone else.

I giggled as Miguel struggled to get the lo mein from his chopsticks into his mouth instead of the usual destination. His lap. The wide grin creased the sexy five o'clock shadow already darkening his face as the food slid off the chopsticks onto the napkin covering his pants. He laid the chopsticks on the placemat and picked up a fork. "I only get an hour for lunch. How do you manage to get the food in your mouth?"

I crossed my chopsticks as though they were swords. "I've had lots of practice. Joy, one of my college roommates, was a navy brat. Her dad was stationed in Taiwan for five years. Every Sunday Joy put all our leftovers into a wok and insisted we eat with chopsticks."

I got up and slid over next to Miguel and put the chopsticks back in his hand. "This isn't brain surgery. A billion Chinese people who are a lot less intelligent than you do this every day. If you are capable of tying your shoelaces, you can do this." I held my chopsticks and took a portion of low main off his plate. "Watch my hands. Rest the bottom stick in the space between your thumb and index finger. The trick is to only move the top stick not the bottom one." I snatched the fork out of his reach and grinned. "If you don't want to starve, then chop-chop."

The server arrived to clear the table and Miguel muttered. "This is an exhausting way to feed yourself. Tacos are a helluva lot easier to eat than this." He brightened and drummed a beat on the edge of the table with his chopsticks. "Speaking of tacos. Jazz Trackers is putting on a concert at Olvera Street this Saturday featuring only Latin jazz musicians. We'll make a day of it. Walk around Olvera Street in the afternoon, and then eat dinner. Joaquin Santos does the best street tacos this side of Tijuana. After we eat, we can take in the outdoor concert at the main plaza in the evening. Sounds great, right?"

Historic Olvera Street is always a kick and Latin jazz is my favorite in the genre. I sighed. "Sounds perfect...but, I'm sorry. I have to pass. I have other plans."

His shoulders slumped. "Bummer. Since Latin jazz is your favorite, I switched weekends with another Captain to get this one free. Is it possible for you to change your plans?"

I said, "It sounds divine and ordinarily, I'd try to, but an old friend from Atlanta is in town, and we're spending the day together."

He asked, "One of your roommates? Which one is she? The nurse or the student?" His eyes widened when I said, "Not she. He. Buddy LaValle."

Miguel smiled, "Try to stay out of trouble for a change."

I batted my eyes. "I resemble the remark, Captain Martinez."

He smirked. "Trouble is your middle name."

I crossed my arms over my chest. "Meaning?"

He pursed his lips. "Josiah Jones is one of my detectives."

Once again, we were off to the races. I jutted my jaw. "And?"

He jutted his jaw further. "And you need to let him do his job."

I shrugged. "Who's stopping him?"

Miguel's obsidian eyes turned hard as diamonds.

"Make sure it isn't you."

Whoa. I narrowed my eyes. "Are you threatening me, Captain?"

He put out his hands. "No, I'm not. But since you insist on sticking your nose into his case, this is just a reminder of which one of you wears the badge and carries the gun."

One more reminder and I'd be telling Captain Miguel Martinez *exactly* where he could shove those chopsticks.

Chapter Thirteen

My wise nana had it right. Nothing turns out the way you think it will. My head spun wildly out of control by the end of my evening with Buddy. His life was a story rivaling a novella on Estrella TV. He dumped his fiancée, married another woman, and started a successful apparel company with her. They had a child, and then the wife and daughter died in a head-on collision. His eyes filled as he handed me the photo of his family. He still wore his wedding band, and my heart clenched. Marie, his wife, was an exotic, raven-haired Cajun beauty, and Justine, his daughter? An adorable toddler, the spitting image of Buddy LaValle. He found the memories too painful for him to remain in Louisiana, so Buddy sold everything he owned and moved west to start his life over. Holy guacamole.

I came away from our reunion with more questions than answers. He might have run across the country to put space between himself and an unspeakable tragedy, but no matter how many miles he ran away from it, his past followed him. A blind guy could see Buddy was still in love with his wife. Does such a thing as a second chance exist? Could I compete with a ghost? Or even want to? And while I'm at it, what about my favorite cop? Would Miguel's badge always come between us? So many questions. So few answers. If I only knew.

****

Monday morning, I headed to Queenie's office for some perspective on my evening with Buddy from someone unfamiliar with him. No one would be more honest, albeit more blunt than Queenie Levine. If anyone could cut through the crap and help me figure it out, Queenie was the one.

She stood arms akimbo outside her closed office door. Did she lock herself out? The notion made me laugh out loud. Not a chance. Telephone, telegraph, tell Queenie. Cable News had nothing on Queenie Levine. Afraid of missing out on some juicy tidbit, she *never* closed her office door, let alone locked it, unless she gossiped about the boss. I sidled over and jerked my chin to her closed door. "Hard to believe you locked yourself out. So, you must have lost your keys."

She rolled her eyes and waved a piece of paper under my nose. "As if. Detective Jones arrived with a search warrant. He's in my office now and when he's done, he's going to search my car and my condo!"

I narrowed my eyes. "What's he searching for?"

Queenie shrugged. "How should I know? He wouldn't tell me a thing. I barely tasted my first sip of coffee before he dropped the warrant on my desk and ordered me out of my office."

I stared at her gape-mouthed. "Did you tell David?"

She crossed her eyes. "Oh, sure. Some help he'd be."

No kidding. The boss had his own problems with Detective Jones. David's interference in Queenie's situation could only make matters worse.

I nodded. "Ok, you're right. So, let's get Mr. Smythe involved to make sure the warrant is Kosher." Before she had a chance to answer, Queenie's office door swung open. The locomotive on two feet strode to Queenie with his hand out. "Ms. Levine, I'll need your car keys."

I almost smacked her as Queenie patted herself down. "Gee, sorry to disappoint you. I don't keep them on me, detective." She pointed to her office." They're in my purse." Antagonizing a freight train with a badge and a gun is as stupid as it gets. Will mouthing off to an already cranky cop get you arrested? Is sarcasm directed at a homicide detective a felonious offense? From the death rays shooting from the detective's angry eyes, Queenie was well on the way to the right to remain silent. I bit back a laugh. As if her being silent for more than a minute was in the cards. Jones rolled his eyes and waved his huge hand towards the open office door.

Jones practically dismantled Queenie's car looking for…who knows what? He slammed down her trunk with such force, it was a wonder it didn't fly off its hinges. Whatever he searched for, he didn't find it. "Ms. Levine," the detective spat Queenie's name out as if it was a chunk of wormy apple. "I'll need to search your house and garage again."

Queenie screwed up her face. "I have a full day of work, Mister Detective. I can't leave the office for a minute to satisfy your little witch-hunt." Queenie defiantly jutted her chin." And if you think I'm handing you the keys to my house without me watching what you do, you've got another thing coming. I've no idea what you're expecting to find, but you'll need to wait till I get home to look for it." Queenie held her hand out. "I'll take my keys back now." Without waiting for him to hand them to her, Queenie snatched the keychain off his fingertips. Jones stared gape-mouthed as Queenie turned on her heel and called over her shoulder. "I'll give you a ring when it's convenient for me to let you invade my privacy."

Queenie swung her arms as she stalked back to the factory. I shivered, imagining the metallic click of the handcuffs as Jones snapped them on her wrists.

****

"Holly Swimsuit!" Buddy shouted into the receiver. "We got us some celebratin' to do!" Saturday night, we clinked a toast with champagne flutes at a cozy table with a breathtaking view of the Pacific Ocean from inside The Lobster Trap, a trendy, elegant restaurant built on a bluff overlooking the Santa Monica pier.

"I can hardly believe it," he said with a sly grin. "Ole Coonass Buddy LaValle from the other LA is gonna be head of design of three divisions for a major apparel company! A southern boy fits into the New Yawk apparel market 'bout as good as a square peg in a round hole. Besides," Buddy laughed, "I really don't love snow." I tried to keep a neutral expression on my face when he added, "Now don't get me wrong, New Yawk has a lot to offer. Broadway, the Statue of Liberty, and Central Park. But New Yawk don't have Holly Swimsuit." As they say in the old south: Well, shut mah mouth.

I kept a wanly supportive expression plastered on my face as he smiled wistfully. "If Marie could only see me now." Buddy changed locations, but he brought Marie with him. My heart squeezed with compassion, but it ached with the sting of reality. Was a future possible with Buddy and me? Maybe, but who wants this kind? This one was not on the rebound. This was the rebound on drugs. Play second fiddle to a man's dead wife? How do you compete with a ghost? I needed some distance between us. It was impossible to breathe, let alone think, with Buddy close enough for me to get heady inhaling his citrusy cologne and touching his cheek. As for going on for the rest of the evening with my emotions careening faster than the Pacific Ocean Park rollercoaster? As if. I feigned a sudden headache and took a raincheck on a nightcap. I dropped him off at the hotel and drove the long way home along the beach to clear my head. The onshore wind gusted in from the ocean. I pulled my jacket tighter, but it didn't help. Maybe the shiver wasn't caused by the wind. Crap. I had to stop answering the phone.

****

Cell phone coverage at the beach is iffy at best with lots of dead spots. So, it was no surprise I'd missed a couple of calls. The fear in Queenie's quivering voice was palatable. "Hol," she whispered the first time. "Call me back when you get this message, it's kinda important." A mixture of terror and annoyance laced her tone by the second call. "Call me for crying out loud! Detective Jones and an army of cops are at my condo taking it apart. I don't know how it ended up in my golf bag, but he's found a syringe in it!" My stomach bounced with a flip flop. Crap, the second message came in over an hour ago. I'm some friend. While I'm glugging expensive champagne, my pal might have been carted off to jail. I sagged with relief when she picked up the receiver. I explained I'd been celebrating with Buddy LaValle and Queenie snapped, "And I'm supposed to know who the hell Buddy LaValle is?"

Mental head slap. Detective Jones derailed my telling her about Buddy with his search of Queenie's office and car, so she was in the dark. It wasn't the right time to go into the saga of Holly Swimsuit and Buddy LaValle, but she asked. I gave her the *Reader's Digest* version and she whistled. "Wow. This is a made-for-TV movie story." Would it be a three-tissue tear-jerker novella with a tragic ending or would we live happily ever after? Flip a coin.

So much for the fairy tale. Now it was time for a real-life drama. I settled in with Siggie snuggled next to me as Queenie related the details of her delightful evening with Detective Jones. I shuddered just listening to her describe the nightmare. For over two hours, Jones and two uniformed patrolmen took her home and garage apart. She got to the part Jones confronted her with the syringe, and I asked, "So they allowed you to keep your cell phone in lockup, or are you out on bail?"

Queenie replied part snort and part cackle. "Oh, believe me." She laughed. "He pulled the handcuffs out, but stopped short of slapping them on my wrists. Finding the syringe is pretty damning, but until he proves it's the one used to shoot the muscle relaxant into Butch, it doesn't mean a thing."

I pursed my lips. "It's time to speak to a lawyer. Call Ms. Markowitz."

When Sonia Wilson was wrongly arrested for buying office executive Bunny Frank's murder, she didn't have a lawyer. I called my Uncle Barry, a personal injury attorney in Beverly Hills for help, and he sang Rose Markowitz's praises. "If I ever found myself in trouble with the law, Rose Markowitz is the one attorney I'd ever call." With complete trust in my uncle, I put Sonia Wilson's life in Ms. Markowitz's hands. Thank God. The diminutive octogenarian criminal defense attorney extraordinaire turned out to be a superstar. She kicked the homicide detective's ass and my colleague was released from jail before the fingerprint ink dried. Ms. M. saved Sonia Wilson's tush. Queenie Levine's tush sure needed some saving right now.

Queenie clucked her tongue. "If you run to a lawyer, it only makes you look more guilty."

I tsked. "And if the tables had been turned, you would have…?"

She laughed out loud. "Taken you by the scruff of your neck, kicking and screaming to Ms. Markowitz's office."

I twirled a ta-da. "Right as rain, kiddo. Consulting a lawyer doesn't make you look guilty. It makes you look smart. No one puts an obstinate detective in their place more thoroughly than Ms. M. If you get her involved now, maybe you nip this in the bud. She gets Jones off your back and focuses on finding the real killer. If heaven forbid, he arrests you, she's already familiar with the case. So, are you gonna do the smart thing or wait and roll the dice to see how stylish you look in handcuffs?"

Chapter Fourteen

Queenie had already downed her second scotch by the time I slid into the seat across from her at Coast Burgers. Siggie settled under the patio table and went to sleep with his head resting on my feet. Queenie and Rose Markowitz met with Detective Jones earlier in the afternoon. Since Queenie sat across from me and wasn't behind bars, I assumed the meeting went ok. We scarfed down our burgers. After I guzzled the second fortifying glass of Chardonnay, Queenie filled me in.

Queenie grinned. "So, I'm in my usual four-inch stilettos, and I struggled to keep pace with the old bird. She'd dressed to the nines for our confrontation, senior citizen comfy style in another killer designer business suit and high-top sneakers." Queenie stood up, threw her shoulders back, jutted her jaw, and strutted the length of the restaurant with a spot-on imitation of the octogenarian dynamo. "With me following behind her with the precision of an obedient baby duckling, our Ms. M stalked confidently into the police station at 3:45 pm as if she owned the place. She shoved her business card under the nose of the desk sergeant, announced us, and asked for Detective Jonesala."

I gawked, "*That's* the way she referred to Detective Jones?"

Queenie smirked. "Bet your sweet ass she did. The cop at the desk gave her a strange look and she giggled like a naughty schoolgirl. She corrected her request with a laugh. 'Oh sorry, I meant a 4:00 with Detective Josiah Jones. Please inform him that Ms. Markowitz and Ms. Levine are waiting.' When the desk sergeant turned his back on us to call the detective, I tugged at Rose's purse and whispered, 'Detective Jonesala? Ms. M, you know this cop?' Rose laughed and patted my arm. She said, 'Know him? Oh yeah, the giant detective and I go way back.' I looked at her wrinkled face and couldn't decide if it meant something good or bad. I soon found out. Precisely at 4:00, Detective Jones's gigantic body filled the open reception room door frame, the same way as in my office. He smiled like a shark as he said his hello to me, but Jones blanched as he noticed Ms. M standing next to me. To say the least, Detective Jones didn't do a happy dance seeing her."

Queenie grinned. "If a black guy can pale, the cop turned ghost-white seeing Ms. M standing next to me." Queenie stood up and demonstrated. "Jones bent in half to shake Rose's hand and squeaked, 'Ms. Markowitz, so nice to see you again,' but he said it in a tone meaning anything but. Truly amazing. This little gnome freaked out the cop so badly he could barely talk. He gulped, 'Follow me.' Jones opened the waiting room door and waved us into the inner sanctum."

I asked, "Was the interview conducted in his office?"

Queenie frowned. "No. To rattle me, Jones ushered us into this dingy interrogation room with dim fluorescent lights, pocked gray linoleum floor, faded prison-gray walls, and a two-way mirror. Rose and I sat on two uncomfortable metal card chairs across from the detective at a battered wood table with a tape recorder and notepad sitting on it. Jones positioned the syringe wrapped in a plastic evidence bag on the table pointing at me in the j'accuse position in front of him."

Queenie shook her head. "Bizarre to say the least. First, we're treated as public enemy number one, then Jones slips into attentive party host mode and says, 'Before we get started, may I offer either of you anything to drink? We have some sludge passing for coffee, but if you'd prefer water or soda, both are available.' " Queenie lifted her half-empty glass of scotch to demonstrate. She rolled her eyes and said, "Jones made a joke! He shrugs and says sorry, no hard stuff. The powers-to-be frown on us serving booze."

Everyone in LA is a wannabe comedian. Even the cops.

Queenie said, "I shook my head no, but then just as the detective turned on the recorder, the gnome stood and wiggled her bony ass. 'Nothing to drink, but these horrible chairs, feh! Ya got something less of a torture chamber chair for an old tush?' "

I choked on my Chardonnay. "I bet he told her it's an interrogation room, not a day at the spa."

Queenie laughed out loud. "No. Jones raised a brow and the corner of his lips quirked a small grin."

I crossed my eyes. "Come on. No way."

She nodded emphatically. "Yeah. Way. Then he picked up the phone and a couple of minutes later, a uniformed cop rolled two torn leather chairs in. Jones grinned as he pointed to the tears in the chairs. 'Sorry about the torn fabric. I hope these meet with your approval, counselor. On such short notice, it's the best I can do.' "

I quipped, "Gee, no footstools?"

Queenie grinned. "No, and Ms. M. needed one. Her feet were a yard shy of touching the floor. Then Jones was all business. He turned on the recorder and stated for the record the time and the date as well as the attendees' names. I squirmed in my seat as he lowered his voice to the level of James Earl Jones. 'Ms. Levine, thank you for you and your counsel volunteering to come in today. Ms. Levine, are you a diabetic?' "

An experienced attorney, Rose Markowitz had prepped Queenie well. Queenie met her before the interview, and Rose instructed her client to think before she responded, not to blurt anything out, to answer the questions honestly. But only answer the question asked, and not to embellish or explain anything. If she was unsure of the question, ask the cop to repeat it, even if a couple of times, until the question was as clear to her as it was to him. Most importantly, Rose instructed Queenie to glance at her lawyer before answering any of the cop's questions to make sure Ms. M. wanted her to respond. If Rose objected, she instructed Queenie not to answer, no matter how belligerent the detective became.

"I glanced at Rose. She nodded ok, so, I said, no I am not." Queenie gulped. "I almost jumped out of my seat when Jones waved the syringe in the evidence bag in my face and snarled, 'Then how do you explain this in your golf bag?' "

I gasped. "Good grief. I would have wet my pants by now. What happened next?"

Queenie clamped her hand around her bicep. "Rose put an arthritic finger on my arm and stabbed me with a nail. So, I kept my lips zipped tight. Rose smiled sweetly at Jones and said, 'You searched my client's office, her car, and her condo, yes?' Without giving Jones a chance to answer, Rose asked, 'Find any other syringes anyplace else in her office, her car, or her condo? Find any insulin? Find any blood testing paraphernalia?' "

By then I hung on Queenie's every word. "She trapped him."

Queenie pursed her lips. "Not in his opinion. Jones smiled like the cat that ate the canary and said, 'No, we didn't find any other syringes, and thanks for making the point.' "

Yikes. Maybe the wily old dame wasn't as sharp as she used to be?

Queenie widened her eyes. "I'm two steps from a fit, but Rose caught his intent and smiled back. Ms. M. said, 'I agree, indeed it is.' " Queenie grinned wider than a carnival barker. "Jones' smile faded as Rose said, 'My client plays golf a couple of times a week and after the game, she and her foursome go into the clubhouse bar while her *unattended* golf bag is out in the slots in front of the course restaurant. *Anyone* could plant the syringe in her bag, and you know it. It would be pretty stupid on her part to hide something so incriminating in her golf bag.' "

Queenie said, "I thought she nailed him, but he smiled and said, 'Well Ms. Markowitz, no one said a killer has to be a genius.' Rose ignored his comment and asked when the syringe would be tested. He said it will be sent to the lab after the interview."

Queenie remarked Rose saw no need to point out the obvious. Until the syringe was tested, Jones couldn't ask any more questions about it. She said he flipped a couple of pages in his notepad and moved on.

Queenie sighed. "Then Jones said, 'Ms. Levine, when I interviewed you in your office, I asked you about your relationship with the victim. Do you recall your response?' I glanced at Rose. She nodded ok, so I answered. 'Yeah. I said I worked for him.' She said Jones smiled smarmily, 'Yes, exactly. But you neglected to share that your relationship with the victim was a lot more, right?' "

I gave Queenie the stink eye. "Ms. M knew *nothing* about your affair with Butch?"

Queenie hung her head. "I know, I know. Pretty stupid. It was too embarrassing to tell her I'd done something so dumb."

I huffed. "Well, not telling her is a helluva lot dumber. I bet she was pissed. It's bad enough getting blindsided by the cops. It's way worse getting blindsided by the client. My Uncle Barry always said the questions you didn't know the answers to are always the ones torpedoing the boat." I clucked my tongue. "So, Albert Einstein, how'd you get yourself out of this one?"

Queenie shrugged. "I leaned over to Rose and whispered the *Reader's Digest* version." Queenie threw up her hands. "Ok, ok, so Rose rolled her eyes and asked why I didn't wait a little longer to get around to telling her?"

I asked, "So which way did she tell you to handle it?"

"To make light of it. So, I giggled and said to the cop, 'Yeah, mea culpa, ya got me. We had a very short affair at the beginning of my stint at Royal Swimwear when I was young and stupid. Who cares about ancient history?' "

I grimaced. "I can only imagine his reaction."

She gulped. "Similar to smelling a fart in church. Jones smacked the table and barked, 'Or, you never got over the affair or the humiliation of his dumping you. Or you were furious he tried to fire you and you struck back.' "

I gulped. "Holy guacamole. Talk about turning your words around."

Queenie nodded. "I whispered to Rose the cop was blowing smoke up my skirt and he knew it. She told me to call him out on it, so I went after him. I said, 'Detective, you know it's a bunch of BS. His attempt to get me fired went no place except to make Butch Oldham look foolish.' "

I asked, "Jones back off?"

Queenie shook her head. "Not on your life. He sneered, 'Oh, come on now, Ms. Levine. You're jilted by a lover. Then he has the nerve to try to get you fired. Whether he succeeded or not is beside the point. You were hurt and then humiliated by the victim twice. You were furious. You made sure he wouldn't do it a third time.' " Queenie clenched her fists. "Rose sensed me ready to reach across the table and slap the SOB. She put two fingers on my arm. She leaned over and whispered the detective is reaching and not to answer. Let the big guy stew in his juices until he parboiled."

I sat on the edge of my seat by then. This story played better than any novella on Estrella TV.

Queenie took a glug of her scotch and said the gnome smiled at the detective. "Jonesala, dahling, the victim was found with cutting shears shoved into his chest." Queenie picked up a butter knife and imitated Rose grimacing and held it over her chest. "Rose said, 'Through the heart too, feh, so messy. Blood everyplace, no? So, you arrived at the crime scene and found my client covered with the victim's blood, right?' " Queenie said Jones shook his head no. She said Ms. M asked the cop, "Don't you find it kinda telling?" Queenie said Jones laughed. "Yeah, it's telling me she washed her hands and changed her clothes." Queenie said Rose never raised her voice. "You've searched her office, her car, and her condo and except for one syringe anyone could plant in her golf bag, ya found zilch. Find any of her fingerprints on the shears or the pins holding down the Vic's extremities?"

I said, "And?"

Queenie said Rose didn't give him a chance to answer. She said Rose reached into her briefcase and pulled out a clear plastic baggie containing the unsigned warning note Queenie received and pushed it over to Jones.

I scoffed, "He wasn't too kicked in the ass the first time you showed it to him, any more than the one I received at the same time. What about the second time?"

Queenie pursed her lips. "Not any better. Rose shook a gnarled index finger at the detective when he rolled his eyes." Queenie said she knew Jones pissed Rose off, but Ms. M. kept her cool. She said Rose snorted, "I understand you accused my client of creating this note herself. I had no idea you possessed such a great sense of humor." Then Rose drilled the cop with a look capable of melting the barrel of his gun. "I don't know, Jonesala. If it's me, just to cover my tush, I would have sent it to the lab for analyzation instead of poo-pooing it. But that's just me." Rose shrugged. "You're the big-time detective, not me."

I widened my eyes. This was not a cop whose competence you questioned and got away with it. "Good grief. What was his reaction to her put-down?"

Queenie grinned evilly. "Jones squirmed in his seat like a truant schoolboy."

"What about," I asked reasonably, "the syringe he found in your golf bag? Isn't it kinda his smoking gun?"

Queenie waved my concern away as though it was a pesky fly at a picnic. "Nah. It would be, but Ms. M pointed out I bought syringes for my sister months before. And besides, if it wasn't my sister's, like Ms. M. said, anyone could plant it. It's at the lab now being tested for content. For all we know, it has plain water." Queenie cackled, "She interrogated him. She made him admit there was no blood on my hands, or my fingerprints anyplace near the crime scene. She shoved the warning note up his ass and made him look like a dope."

I wrinkled my forehead. "And if the test comes back on the syringe proving a muscle relaxer is in it?"

Queenie shrugged. "I guess he'll still need to prove I put it in the syringe and I shot Butch up using it." Queenie leaned back in her seat and dangled her legs to demonstrate. She said, "Rose sat in a pretty deep leather chair, and her feet were far from touching the floor. Jones smiled, amused as he watched her struggle to get out of the seat. When Rose finally stood up, her chest was almost level with the table. She shouldered her purse and looked up at Jones. Rose grinned. 'Jonesala, great seeing you again. This has been mildly entertaining. Let's do lunch soon, my treat.' She tore him apart and then Rose shot Jones with a look pinning him to his chair. She laughed. 'I'm kinda disappointed. I thought you had something more than fairy tales to share. If you manage to find one shred of proof to all your silly theories, give my office a call. Until then, this meeting is over.' She gave my arm a surprisingly strong yank. Then she picked up her heavy briefcase she must carry bricks inside and pulled me by the arm. I followed her out like an obedient puppy and we walked out the door."

Queenie laughed out loud. "What a pleasure it was seeing her in action. Standing next to him, she barely came up to his waist! He could probably crush her in the palm of his hand if he wanted to, but by the end of the meeting, she maneuvered him to exactly the place she wanted him. He asked me a couple of tough questions, and she responded to most of them."

I took another sip of wine. "Well, it sounds as if you're in the clear, thank God, but I must tell you, for some stupid reason I still feel like I'm missing something obvious. Something is rolling around in my brain, but it won't come to the surface and it's driving me nuts."

Queenie grinned as she pointed to my near-empty wineglass. "You're probably gonna need a lot more wine."

Chapter Fifteen

The moment I drove into the Mermaid Swimwear parking lot, my innards twisted around like a slinky. Six LAPD squad cars parked haphazardly in front of the main entrance. I cut around the cop cars, pulled into my slot, and put the top up on the convertible. I opened the front door of the factory with the same level of caution as the bomb squad defusing an unmarked package. David's secretary, Harriet Cowan, stood at the end of the entrance where the aisles to the executive and design wings converged with the lobby. I waved good morning and turned left to the executive aisle, but Harriet put out a palm to stop me. "You can't go inside."

I gave her the big eyes. "Why?"

Harriet said, "I've been instructed to direct everyone to wait in the lunchroom."

I asked, "By who?"

Harriet pointed to the squad cars outside the front window. "The police."

"I'm gonna take a wild guess they're not collecting donations for the policeman's ball." Visions of Queenie in handcuffs danced in my head. "Are they arresting someone?"

Harriet gulped. "Not yet. Detective Jones and the uniforms stormed into the lobby an hour ago with a warrant permitting them to search both the factory and the warehouse."

I asked, "What are they searching for?"

She shrugged. "No clue. The search warrant wasn't specific. It just gave them the right to search anyplace on the grounds and confiscate anything deemed relevant to the case. Two uniforms are in the executive and design wings and four are in the warehouse."

Our factory is a substantial-sized building, but the warehouse attached to it occupied an entire city block. Between the production and shipping teams, over one hundred employees worked in the warehouse. The lunchroom is a huge room, but it wasn't big enough to accommodate all the employees at the same time.

I snorted. "And Detective Jones expected *all* our employees to fit into the lunchroom?"

Harriet shook her head. "I brought the detective to the lunchroom so he could see for himself that it wouldn't accommodate us all. We sent the warehouse people outside on the loading dock and the factory people to the lunchroom. It's crowded but it'll work."

Holy guacamole. "Did the detective say how long this is gonna take? I have a presentation half-completed. It's gotta ship this afternoon to Bullseye Stores for a style meeting tomorrow morning. If we miss the meeting, we won't get any first-quarter purchase orders."

Harriet shook her head. "Nope. They'll inform me when they're finished. Do me a favor. Make sure enough coffee is brewed, so the natives don't get too restless."

Normally a hotbed of gossip and gab, the packed to maximum capacity Mermaid lunchroom with anxious employees was eerily quiet as a church during Sunday services. The only sound was the perking third pot of fresh coffee I'd brewed. The tension exacerbated by the fear of a murder investigation was thick enough to cut with a dull knife. Mostly heads down, the group kept their thoughts and fears to themselves. I took the temperature of the crowd with furtive glances around. Red hot. I checked the time and the supply of coffee. We were running out of both.

I'd just poured the bazzillionth cup of coffee that neither Queenie nor I wanted, but we took just for something to do with our hands when Detective Jones's massive body filled the entrance to the lunchroom. Every head in the room turned and faced the cop.

He said, "Our search of the premises is complete. Thank you for your patience and cooperation. You're all free to go back to your work areas." The crowd made a mass exodus for the door, but Jones blocked the way out. The cop put out a hand as though directing rush hour traffic and glared at Queenie. "I'm sorry, let me revise my announcement." Jones waved a clear evidence bag with her blood-stained sweater inside like the bait for a mousetrap under Queenie's nose. She squeezed my hand so tightly it's a wonder I still had working fingers when Jones lasered his eyes at Queenie and glared. "All *but* Ms. Levine are free to leave."

****

Word of high-profile player Queenie Levine's arrest spread through the swimwear industry with the speed of a wildfire. The buzz of conversation at A Jolt of Java stopped as a dozen sets of eyes followed me from the barista station to the Yenta table the next morning. I kept my sunglasses on and slunk down in my seat to avoid the inevitable throngs of nosy looky-loos. Joan observed me over the top of her eyeglasses. "Listen, Greta Garbo, if you're going for inconspicuous, the only thing those sunglasses do is make you stick out big as a sore thumb."

I snatched the sunglasses off my nose and shoved them into the hobo bag. I glugged a restorative half a cup of coffee and faced my friends. The chair Queenie normally occupied across from me sat as empty as our hearts. Each of us brought something special to the Yentas. If Joan brought the spice to the group, Queenie is the determined spirit who never lets us forget to fight for what we believe in.

Joan asked, "You were in the lunchroom when she was arrested?"

I nodded numbly. Queenie shackled by handcuffs is an image forever branded into my memory. "Jones told everyone but Queenie they could leave. I walked out with the rest of the group, but I hung back. The lunchroom door stayed open, so I stood to the side and eavesdropped. I angled my head to see in, but they sat at the table in the back of the lunchroom and didn't see me. Jones laid the evidence bag with Queenie's sweater in it on the table."

I surveyed the table. "You guys know the sweater is Queenie's pride and joy. She was so upset it went missing the day of the murder. My heart broke at Queenie's reaction. She got so excited it was found, the implication went over her head." My voice caught. "She squealed. Oh my God. You found my lucky sweater. Thank you so much, detective. She asked, where in the world was it?"

Hope sucked in her cheeks. "Is she blind? The bloodstains should have been her first clue."

I shook my head. "It wasn't out of the evidence bag yet. So, Jones puts on surgical gloves and takes the sweater out, and unfolds it. The sweater's real color is white, but the dried blood stained it a rusty brown.

Queenie reaches for the sweater and shrieks oh my God, what happened to it? It's ruined. Jones snatches the sweater away before Queenie touches it and puts it back in the evidence bag. Jones says, you know what it is. It's blood. The blood of the victim you killed and maybe even yours. He sneered, we found it in the place you hid it after you killed him. After you murdered your boss in cold blood, you hid the bloody sweater. Queenie gives him a look as though he's lost his mind and says I didn't kill anyone or hide the sweater anyplace. I've torn the building apart looking for it."

Joan asks, "So, what was the detective's response?"

I shuddered. "He said, stand up and put your hands behind your back, Ms. Levine. You're under arrest for the murder of Benjamin Oldham. He cuffed her and read her the rights." I grimaced, "I stood in front of them and blocked the way without worrying if the cop was pissed at me or not. I ignored him and looked her in the eye. I said, Do. Not. Say. Another. Word. Do. You. Hear. Me? No matter what he says or asks, do not respond. No matter what he does, do not react. Your lawyer will meet you at the station."

Joan looked over her glasses. "She understood your instructions?"

"She nodded yes. Jones perp-walked her through the hordes of employees staring gape-mouthed at the spectacle and lead her out of the building. I ran to my office and called Ms. Markowitz. Then I filled David and Mr. Smythe in."

Hope asked, "When your boss was accused of murdering Jack Tyne, the company hired his criminal attorney for him, right?"

I nodded, "The company has an insurance policy for

top senior execs which includes legal counsel, but we aren't high enough in the pecking order to qualify. Besides," I grinned, "I can hardly wait to see midget Markowitz cut giant Josiah Jones down to size."

Hope's red-rimmed eyes blinked at the unshed tears. "Did they let you see her?"

I shook my head no. "They gave me the same runaround as the last time. Only counsel is allowed to see prisoners."

Sonia asked, "Did you see Ms. Markowitz?"

I nodded yes. "I met Ms. Markowitz at her office after she saw Queenie."

Sonia sucked in her cheeks. "How is Queenie?"

Hope shivered. "She must be terrified."

I grinned. "She told Ms. Markowitz to get her out fast as orange is not her best color."

Joan grimaced. "What evidence does the detective have on our girl?"

My grin faded to a grim sigh. "No smoking gun, but more than enough to get her arrested. Jones interviewed Queenie's cousin Arnie Levine who is a pharmacist. The cousin admitted Queenie purchased syringes from him a couple of months ago."

Hope asked, "How come Queenie knew the cop interviewed her cousin?"

"Her cousin called her and gave her a heads up."

Sonia furrowed her brow. "She's diabetic?"

I shook my head. "She's not."

Joan narrowed her eyes. "If she's not diabetic, why does she need syringes? It might be innocent, but it looks pretty darned suspicious given the way Butch was drugged."

I said, "Queenie's sister Laura is diabetic. She

visited from Florida over the holidays and ran out of syringes, so Queenie bought her an emergency supply. Laura and Queenie played golf a few times. Queenie said it must be how the syringe got into her golf bag. Her cousin the pharmacist knew all this, but failed to share it with the cop."

Joan clucked her tongue. "So, are you saying the detective thinks Queenie bought syringes months ago to murder Butch now? Makes no sense. If murdering Butch is the reason she bought the syringe, why not do the deed right then?"

I shrugged. "We'll never have the answer to the question. The cop's evidence was circumstantial when he interviewed Queenie, with no smoking gun. Ms. Markowitz dispelled most of it and we thought Queenie was home free. But added to however, and whenever the syringe got into her golf bag, her muscle relaxant, her hatred of Butch, blaming him for the bankruptcy, the threats she made saying she would make sure Butch got everything he deserved, and their ill-fated affair was all bad enough. But the bloody sweater *is* the smoking gun, and it nailed her. If Queenie's blood is on it or the shears, she's toast."

Sonia pursed her lips. "Our girl is innocent, but somebody killed Butch. Who?"

Joan screwed up her face and spat. "Butch was a conniving, gold medal champion when it came to screwing you out of something. Butch Oldham didn't have an honest bone in his twerpy little body." Our Joan was right, but her experience with Butch influenced her opinion with the stain of prejudice. Joan was the Royal Swimwear showroom manager for twenty years. The original owner of the company sold it to a mega-conglomerate, and they hired Butch to run the operation. Butch's daughter Lauren convinced him to fire old-school Joan and hire her BFF Lissa Charney. Joan reinvented herself and became an independent sales rep. Lissa was murdered and Joan was wrongly accused of the crime. Even though Joan was exonerated, no love was lost between Butch and Joan." Joan blushed. "It's a good thing I had back-to-back appointments in San Diego the day Butch got killed, or I'd be a prime suspect."

Hope looked at Joan and asked, "Ok, so it's not you or Queenie. So, who?"

Sonia drummed a beat on the table with a spoon. "Who are the ones this man harmed the most?"

I said, "David and Butch's wife Kelly…."

Joan pinched her lips. "Ok, Nancy Drew. A but is coming next, right?"

I grinned. "David and Kelly? The most harmed, *but…* they both got what they wanted, if not expected, from Butch. They have no motive."

Joan shrugged, "Remember, the cops on TV always say…?"

We chorused, "Follow the money."

Chapter Sixteen

Calling Queenie to discuss a problem? As natural as breathing out and breathing in. I dialed her extension and drummed my fingers impatiently on my desk. Answer already, for crying out loud. This is freaking important. Where the Sam Hill could she be? Good grief. She pissed me off more with each ring. It took six rings before it occurred to me why Queenie hadn't picked up the phone. With the click of a set of handcuffs, suddenly I'm Starsky without Hutch. Sherlock without Watson. Nick Charles without Nora. Hercule Poirot without Arthur Hastings…in other words, I was all on my own. It is true. You don't know what you've got until it's gone. I needed help. I needed some perspective. My go-to-gal was unavailable. I dialed the only other person who might be able to help.

Four rings and an official-sounding voice greeted me. "Los Angeles County Medical Examiner's office. Dr. Sophie Cutler speaking. You stab 'em, we slab 'em."

I laughed. "Caller ID has changed your life, hasn't it?"

My favorite coroner joshed, "It's the real reason I come to work every day. How may I help you today? I hate to rush you along, but I'm up to my elbows in a patient's chest cavity right now. As much as I'd love to chat, please make it snappy. I better get back to him before his esophagus seizes."

Eek. My stomach turned at the image. Of course, the sight of a squashed bug makes me queasy. And she does this every day? Better her than me. Nonetheless, before she dismissed me, I got right to it. "Ok, just answer one question. Are the test results on Queenie's sweater, the shears, and the eye pins back yet?"

Doctor picky perfectionist replied, "Technically, you asked three questions, but who's counting? Lucky for you, your timing is good. I just received the preliminary reports back an hour ago. Two sets of bloodstains are on the sweater. The front of the sweater is permeated with the most common blood type, O positive. The blood is from a male. The Sleeves are drenched with a mixture of O positive and AB negative blood, the rarest blood type. The AB negative blood is from a female. Fingerprints on the sweater buttons belong to a female. The blades of the shears: blood is type O positive. The handles: type O positive mixed with type AB negative. Eye pins: pinpoints type O positive. Eyes: O positive mixed with type AB negative."

I said, "So, Butch was type O?"

Snip said, "Yes."

I crossed my fingers and prayed. "Based on the blood type, the killer could be a man or a woman."

My heart sank as she sighed with the weariness of someone who always delivered bad news. "Nope. The killer is a female."

A conversation with Butch's secretary earlier flitted across my memory. I perked up. "Run Mariana Green's blood type and prints through the system and see if she's a match. She was initially arrested along with Dick. Even though she'd been cleared and released, she must still be in the system. I've spoken to her and she blames Butch for her husband's fall from grace. If you remember, she works out at a gym and uses muscle relaxants. Butch's secretary Helen mentioned Mariana was at the Mermaid factory the day of the murder collecting her husband's personal effects. Dick's office is right next to Butch's. Maybe his wife confronted Butch, it turned ugly, and in a rage, she killed him."

Doctor Death quickly struck down my next idea. "It's a long shot. Even if it's a match, explaining the bloody sweater will be a challenge."

Not so fast, sister. Not necessarily so. "Why? Queenie's office is across the hall from Dick's. Queenie never locks her office door, so anyone could go in. The same as the rest of us, Queenie isn't tied to her desk from nine to five. During the day, she's in the design studio, the patternmaking department, the customer service room, the warehouse. She's all over the factory, as well as at the mart. Maybe she was in the meeting with Gary and me in the design studio while Mariana went into Dick's office? I'll ask Helen what time Mariana was in the factory if it helps with a timeline. Mariana sticks her head in Queenie's open door, sees the office is empty, sees Queenie's sweater on the door hook, and grabs it. She confronts Butch, kills him, and uses the bloody sweater to frame Queenie."

Snip blew out a long breath. "I suppose it's possible. I'll run her through the system and see. Your friend Queenie volunteered a blood sample. I'll let you know if it's type AB negative. We'll run the DNA through the system to see if it's a match."

Queenie never had so much as a parking ticket. "I don't know her blood type, but she's never been in trouble with the law, so I doubt you'll find her matching in the system."

Snip asked, "Was your friend ever in the military? If she was, she'll be in the system."

I burst out laughing. As if. I'd pay a king's ransom to see Fashionista Queenie Levine in fatigues and combat boots marching in formation before dawn.

Snip said, "Her fingerprints were taken after she was booked. The sweater is hers, so, her fingerprints are on the buttons. If they match the ones on the eye pins and shears, she's toast." The laughter died in my throat.

Since Snip narrowed the field of suspects by eliminating men as potential candidates, that left Dick Green and David Workman out of the running. And the women? It all still came down to who was harmed the most.

Mariana Green? She certainly had the motive and possibly the means and opportunity. Dick's wife was worth a second visit.

Diane Gentry? She might be diabetic, but Diane beat Butch at his own game and stole his wife. Did it qualify as a motive? Who knew? Still, she might have the means, but what about the opportunity? She and Butch were on the outs. I couldn't imagine a reason why, but maybe Diane was at the factory the day of the murder? I didn't remember seeing her, but someone else might have. I will ask around. I took an imaginary golf swing. This was the perfect time to start my lessons.

Mariana and Diane were two worthy candidates. But no matter which way the cards were shuffled, in the game of who'd been harmed most, Kelly Oldham's card always rose to the top of the deck.

My dialing finger itched with three appointments to make.

Chapter Seventeen

The next afternoon, Bernice, our head patternmaker, gave me the last samples for the Swimsuit Barn presentation. I tagged and hung the samples and printed the line list. Then I took the completed presentation to the shipping department and said a little prayer over the carton after the packing clerk sealed it. I went back to my office and checked the calendar. Hot diggity. Nothing else was on my schedule for the rest of the day. Before David or anyone else waylaid me, I packed my messenger bag and got out of Dodge while the westbound beach traffic still only slowed to a crawl and was not yet at a standstill.

I hadn't spent much time with Siggie the last few days and decided to pamper my pup. I changed into sweats and sneakers after I got back to the houseboat and chose the perfect destination for a nice relaxing walk. Siggie snatched the guilty mom bribery treats out of my hand with a single slurp of his wet tongue. I dangled his leash in front of him. "Ready to stretch your four legs, big guy?" Siggie stood on his hind paws and danced in a happy circle. "WOOF!" I opened the cabin door and he took a flying leap over the forward deck rail and landed effortlessly on the dock. I locked up, hoisted myself over the rail, and snapped the leash on Siggie's collar.

Spring weather at the beach was always a mixed bag. Optimists preferred to say the season has something for everyone. Cool nights with chilly winds blowing the fog in at dawn and dusk, with sunny afternoons and daytime temperatures on the mild side. I shivered into my jacket when the onshore wind made my eyes tear as we bisected the marina and walked toward the main channel entrance on the western side. "Siggie, Kelly Oldham should be our number one suspect, but my gut tells me Mariana Green is our killer. Do you agree?"

"Woof, woof."

"Ok good. Glad you agree. Her boat is moored on the other side of the marina. Let's go by and see what we can see."

"Woof."

Mariana and Dick's yacht, *By the Numbers* sat moored in the next to last basin before the main channel. I opened the gate with my security key and we walked down the gangplank. I stopped dead in my tracks halfway to their slip. The last two people in the world I expected to see on the aft deck of Dick Green's boat swigging beer were Kelly Oldham and Diane Gentry.

Kelly sprang back to her gorgeous self. Her complexion was no longer the color of wet cement and her eyes were not red from crying. Decked out in a skimpy bikini leaving *nothing* to the imagination, Kelly Oldham's period of grieving her husband's murder was over and done.

In case they saw us, I resisted the urge to point. "Siggie, why are Kelly and Diane on Dick Green's boat?"

"Woof."

"Maybe they bought the boat?"

"Woof, woof."

"No other explanation makes sense, right?"

"Woof."

"Yes, of course, you're right. The only way to find out is to ask them."

We sidled over to Dick Green's slip, and I rapped three sharp knocks on the forward rail. "Ahoy, permission to board requested."

Diane toasted me with her beer and burst out laughing. "Who are you supposed to be? Admiral Halsey in drag?"

I swept an arm around the marina. "If you're gonna own a boat, you might want to familiarize yourself with the nautical protocols."

Diane poked an index finger into her chest and looked at me wonky. "Own a boat? Who, me?"

I gave Kelly a two-finger salute and pointed to the beer. "Well, you two look as though you've made yourselves at home, so I figured you bought the boat and are hanging out." I craned my neck around from the bow to the stern, looking for Mariana, but she was not on the deck. "Is Mariana below?"

Kelly smiled wanly. "No on both counts. We didn't buy the boat and you missed Mariana by about an hour and a half."

I crossed my fingers behind my back and lied through my teeth. "Too bad. I hoped to catch her. She said she'd be aboard most days this week and I came over to see if she wanted to grab a bite."

Kelly narrowed her eyes. "What makes you think I could afford a yacht, even if I wanted to buy it?"

I ignored her question and asked one of my own. "Then why are you aboard, if you don't mind me asking?"

Before she replied, Siggie grew tired of standing

around listening to us yammering and decided to jump onto the boat. Kelly found it utterly hysterical as Diane shrank back in fear watching my oversized four-legged bundle of joy fill the space between her and the forward door. Without waiting for permission to board, I climbed the three-step ladder and hoisted myself over the aft deck railing. I gave my big boy a couple of love scratches behind his ears. "Don't worry. He's a lover, not a fighter."

Diane grabbed a beer from inside a cooler and held it out as a peace offering. "Want a cold brewski?"

I pulled the travel doggie water cup out of my jacket pocket and pointed to my pooch. "Sure. And Siggie is thirsty too."

Diane almost jumped over the railing when Siggie barked, "Woof!" Diane narrowed her eyes. "You let him drink beer?"

I crossed my eyes and held out his bowl. "Nope. He's a teetotaler. Plain water will suit him fine, please."

Diane held out a trembling hand and wiggled her index finger at Siggie's bowl. "Better give me his dish now."

She took a bottle of water out of the cooler and filled Siggie's bowl to the brim. She cautiously set it on the deck in front of him and quickly snatched her hand away as he stuck his big head into the bowl.

I popped the top of the beer and guzzled a swig. "So, how come you're aboard?"

Diane said, "Mariana accepted an offer last night and the guy wants the boat by the end of the week. She needed to get it cleaned out pronto. With a boat this size, it's too a big a job for one person, so we volunteered to help her. Even with three of us, it took over four hours, but we only got half of it done. We have to come back again sometime this week to finish cleaning the boat out once she confirms which day the transfer will take place. She's meeting the buyer now to finalize the terms of the deal." Diane rattled a keyring. "She gave us the key and said to hang out as long as we wanted and just give her the key before we play golf Friday morning."

I did a mental double-take. Play golf? Together? Talk about strange bedfellows. "I had no idea you guys even knew one another."

Kelly said, "We met at the Mermaid Christmas party and Diane and Mariana hit it off." Diane smiled wickedly. "We discovered a couple of common interests. We both love to play golf and hate Butch Oldham. You'll probably see her after our lesson Sunday. We're part of a foursome with a tee time after lunch."

"After one of their games, they met me for lunch at the café inside the Bainbridge Department Store in the Westside Pavilions Mall." Kelly giggled. "Diane would rather eat snails than go shopping with me. She ran away as if her pants had been set on fire when I said I wanted to go to Bainbridge for their half-yearly sale. Mariana loves bargain hunting and we had a blast. We bought some fabulous things for a song and got to know one another. Turns out she loves to shop as much as I do. We meet for lunch once a week and then go to a different mall." Kelly smiled. "Mariana is almost old enough to be my mother and she's sort of adopted me. I'm the daughter she always wanted. She's been trying to teach me to play mahjong." Kelly hung her head. "It's not going well. No matter how many times she goes over it, I can't tell one tile from another." Kelly grinned. "We're gonna ditch the mahjong lessons and stick to something

I'm better at…"

Diane fondly cuffed Kelly's shoulder and smirked. "Spending money?"

Chapter Eighteen

Since I missed her on the boat, I called Mariana the next day and asked to stop by after work. She agreed but oddly, never asked the purpose of my visit. Traffic over the hill was bumper to bumper and the trip took much longer than expected. With no places to stop once I drove deep into the canyon, I needed to wiz something fierce by the time I arrived at Mariana's house. I barely said hello and ran for the powder room. After I peed, I checked the medicine chest. Same stuff as last time. Dang it.

I returned to the living room and once again sunk up to my neck on the man-eating sofa. I rearranged myself on the squishy cushions to face my hostess and grinned. "Ah, much better." I meant it when I said, "Congratulations on selling your boat. The word around the marina is it's a buyer's market. All the yacht dealers are complaining loudly. Did you get the price you asked for or need to drop it?"

She smiled. "It is a buyer's market but I caught a lucky break. There's a huge demand for our size boat, but no available inventory. Two buyers were locked in a bidding war. Three days after the ad ran, I accepted an offer at twenty grand more than I listed the boat for."

I widened my eyes. "You could have knocked me over with a feather finding Kelly and Diane chilling out on your boat. I didn't realize you three even knew one another."

Mariana grinned. "Yeah, we were friendly before, but the last few weeks? Let's just say we've become a lot closer."

Mariana smirked as she eyed me over the rim of her teacup. "Come over for another tea party?"

As if. The good manners Nana raised me with were the only reason I accepted a cup of the brew. I drank about a quarter of the swill to be polite and tried not to gag. Less bitter than the last time but with a slight metallic taste. It was certainly not an improvement. Maybe my tastebuds protested the tea, or she changed brands? The tea party concluded after I put the teacup back on the table. Time to get to the point. "I'm investigating Butch Oldham's murder."

She blinked her confusion. "Nothing to investigate. The police arrested the bastard's killer."

I shook my head. "They arrested a *suspect*, but not the *killer*. We both know Queenie didn't kill him."

Mariana scoffed. "I know no such thing. The word is the cops say it's an open and shut case. Your friend did the world a favor by taking the SOB out. She deserves a reward."

I gave her the stink eye. "BS. Their case has more holes in it than Swiss cheese, and I'm gonna prove it. Detective Jones stopped asking, but I have some questions."

She batted her eyes. "You can ask all your questions, but I doubt I will have any answers."

I said, "You were at the Mermaid factory the day of the murder. Why?"

She shrugged her indifference. "What of it? I went to get Dick's personal belongings out of his office."

I narrowed my eyes. "You don't live close to the Mermaid facility. Why go all the way to the factory? Why not let Dick's secretary pack his stuff and ship it to your house?"

She scoffed with derision. "As if I would trust anyone at Mermaid Swimwear for anything."

I said, "Dick's office is conveniently located next to Butch's."

Her laugh rivaled the bitterness of the tea. "Let me assure you, I didn't go in to say hello."

I tapped the face of my watch. "What time were you at the factory?"

She had a deer in the headlights hesitation. Apparently, she needed to buy some time to pull the answer out of her ass. "Uh, I-I dunno the exact time. S-Sometime after lunch. Why?"

I waved my watch in the air. "You're giving an awfully wide timeline. Could you be more specific?"

She scowled. "I ran some errands after lunch and went there on the way home."

And what way does that shorten the timeline? "How much later after lunch?"

She flicked her wrist. "A couple of hours. Maybe two or three."

I pressed her. "So, around three?"

She shrugged. "Not sure. Maybe."

"How long were you at the factory?"

She sucked in her cheeks. "I dunno. Not long. I arrived. They let me into Dick's office. I collected his stuff, threw it in a carton, and left." She puckered her lips. "I had no desire to hang around. Being in the same building as the monster gave me the willies. I couldn't get out of the place fast enough."

I opened my mouth to ask the next question, but an inexplicable jaw-cracking yawn came out instead.

Mariana snorted. "Are my answers boring you?"

I shook my head. "Sorry to be so rude. It was a long day. Guess it's catching up with me." I stifled another yawn with a self-deprecating grin and focused on the next question. "Did you speak with anyone while you were at Mermaid?"

She scrunched her eyes closed. "Only the receptionist in the lobby and Butch's secretary. She unlocked Dick's office door and re-locked it after I finished getting Dick's stuff out."

"No one other than those two?"

Mariana shook her head no. "Nope."

Her story didn't pass the sniff test. "Human resources have strict protocols regarding the removal of property. Yet, no one called security to examine the box, inventory the contents, make sure you signed the release form, give you a copy, and escort you out of the building?"

She crossed her arms over her chest. "Nope."

I narrowed my eyes. "Pretty hard to believe." I covered my mouth to conceal a yawn wide enough to accommodate a locomotive. Good grief. I slept soundly the night before. Why the Sam Hill was I so drowsy?

She ignored my yawn and gave me the stink eye. "Believe what you want. The welcome wagon wasn't at the front door to greet me when I arrived, but nobody checked the box or walked me out."

I gave her the stink eye back. "So, without a copy of the release form, you've no way to prove how long you were on the premises or why, what you did or took, or which parts of the building you visited."

She spoke through clenched teeth. "I told you. I went into Dick's office, threw all of his crap in a carton, and left the building. Nothing more. Nothing less."

I dipped my head. "Or, the opportunity to get in Butch's face presented itself. You followed him to the warehouse and confronted him. You blamed Butch for all Dick's troubles. He threw Dick under the bus. Your husband is rotting in jail and Butch got away with stealing the company blind. Now you had the chance to punish Butch for destroying Dick." I pointed my index finger in her face J'accuse style. "You called him out. Butch laughed in your face. He called Dick a gullible pencil neck who got what he deserved. You went crazy. You grabbed the nearest weapon. Fabric shears laying on a cutting table. And stabbed Butch in the heart."

She recoiled as though she was struck. "You're out of your mind. The police interviewed me and arrested somebody else." She jutted her chin. "I owe you nothing. I don't have to answer your questions."

I nodded my agreement. "You certainly don't. But you'd look guilty as hell by refusing." Without giving her a chance to argue or throw me out of the house, I changed the direction of my questions. "What's your blood type?"

Mariana widened her eyes and scoffed. "Why? You need a transfusion?"

I snapped, "Cut the sarcasm and answer the question."

She clucked her tongue. "Type O."

The pulse roared in my ears. "Your blood type is all over the crime scene."

She spat. "Mine and a third of mankind's."

Regrettably, it was impossible to argue. I'd run out

of questions and ideas. The only thing I had left was plenty of yawns. My brain turned to mush. It was a long, challenging day. I needed to fetch my pooch from his playday with Peso, grab a takeaway pizza, and then get horizontal. Mariana walked me to the door and said she'd be at her boat the rest of the week if I had any other crazy questions. Cripes.

****

The 405 freeway and the canyon ran north-south and parallel to one another. The freeway was further due west and the more direct route to the beach, but at rush hour it took a while to get from the canyon to the highway. By the time you got onto the 405, both directions were always a nightmare. By comparison, traffic in the canyon would be going the opposite direction than me. So, over the hill was the faster way to the west side at that time of day.

I merged onto Coldwater Canyon going south from Mariana's narrow side street. As I descended from the summit, the downgrade of the canyon road was gradual but became sharply steeper the further south I drove. Exhaustion hit me like a ton of bricks as the car leaned into the first S-turn. It was hard to keep my eyes open. The night turned chilly and my thin windbreaker over a short-sleeved cotton shirt was not doing much to keep me warm. Then I remembered a trick my dad taught me about the best way to stay awake at the wheel. I pulled over onto a gravel-pitted shoulder and put the top down on the convertible. I set the radio volume to wake the dead level and shivered as I merged back onto the two-lane canyon road.

As I turned into the next series of down-draft S-curves, fingers of thick, blinding fog reached into the

132

depths of the canyon floor and wrapped themselves around the car so completely, that I couldn't see my hand in front of my nose. I misjudged the angle of the turn and hit the brake too hard as the car careened around the curve. The car skidded to the side of the cliff and fishtailed on the gravel into the berm. Then the world went black.

Chapter Nineteen

Joan concealed her alarm behind a snappy comment, but the catch in her voice betrayed her. "Does the other guy look any better, or is he worse off than you?"

I winced as I touched the golf ball-sized lump on my forehead. "You're as funny as a lobotomy. Lady Luck wrapped her arms around me. Another five yards to the right, and the cop said I'd have run out of the berm and gone over the cliff. "

Sonia said, "It's not as if you've never driven the canyon before. Don't you take Coldwater Canyon when you visit your friend Chris in the valley?"

A shooting pain zapped me behind the eyes as I nodded my agreement. "You're right. If I'm going to the valley from the west side of town, I go over the canyon route. Rush hour traffic clogs both sides of the 405, but the canyon traffic was only northbound. The canyon wasn't the most direct route, but going south, it's a lot faster to take it into town and cut across the city via an east-west surface street until you get to the beach."

Hope asked, "So, how'd the accident happen? Some speeding nutcase run you off the road? I read an article about the problem in the Times a few weeks ago. Recently, there has been a rash of speeding canyon drivers running other cars off the road and causing several fatal accidents."

I shook my head no. "No, thank goodness. Only a

couple of southbound cars were on my side of the road at the time. Everyone else drove northbound from town into the valley. I went around an S-curve going downhill, and I hit some thick fog. The fog was so dense, that it was impossible to accurately gauge the sharpness of the curve. I misjudged the curve then overcompensated and hit the brakes too hard. The car fishtailed and swerved, and the next thing I knew a cop shined a flashlight into the car and asked if I was ok. I turned my head to look at him, and I saw stars. It was as if somebody took a jackhammer and pounded on the top of my head. The cop asked if I was able to move. I wiggled my fingers and tapped my feet on the floorboard and said yes. The cop opened the car door and I staggered out. I was dizzy from the bang on my noggin. I failed the touching my nose and walking part of the sobriety test. I blew into the breathalyzer, and of course, it registered zero alcohol level."

Sonia asked, "You said you became quite tired and put the top down to stay awake. You fell asleep at the wheel?"

I said, "I won't have the answer for another couple of days."

Three sets of Yenta heads swiveled in my direction and gave me the big eyes.

I explained. "No liquor was ingested, so I wasn't drunk. But since I staggered around as if loaded on something, the cops insisted on me submitting to a drug test. An ambulance took me to Cedars and I called Snip to meet me. They checked me for a concussion and ran a series of drug tests, but the results won't be ready for forty-eight hours." I grinned. "Snip pitched a fit, but it turns out that unless I died, she lacked the authority to put a rush on the tests."

Hope asked, "So, was the night in the hospital ok? I hear Cedars serves gourmet meals."

I said, "No overnight stay, but with my head injury, if Snip didn't take me to her house and continuously monitor me for signs of a concussion, they wouldn't have released me."

Joan widened her eyes. "Your LAPD pals must post your picture on their most wanted list."

I sighed. "Suffice it to say I won't be attending the LAPD charity ball. Detective Jones is ready to arrest me and Miguel isn't arguing."

Sonia asked, "So, why aren't you behind bars? I guess your pal AJ talked them out of it."

I choked on my coffee." Not on your life. Miguel has been pressuring her to help rein me in. If anything, I'm making her look bad to the boss. She's more pissed at me now than Miguel or Jones. If it was up to her, I'd be in the cell next to Queenie. But since Mariana Green refused to file a harassment complaint, they had nothing to charge me with other than being a nosy parker. Miguel isn't answering my calls and AJ barely talked to me when I picked Siggie up the next afternoon."

Joan tapped her upper lip. "Begs the question why Mariana hasn't filed a complaint?"

Sonia smiled sweetly. "Because a guilty person doesn't want to give the cops any reason to dig into their activities."

Hope squeezed her index finger and thumb an inch or so apart. "You came this close to dying this time. Maybe it's a sign for you to back off and let the professionals handle this."

I dipped a shoulder "I don't see how I can. Jones

isn't looking at anyone else. If I don't flush out the killer, Queenie might spend the rest of her life in jail. We all know she is innocent." I squared my shoulders. "Nope, I have to keep going. I'm close to solving this one. I feel it in my bones. And we'll find out soon enough if I'm right."

The Yentas chorused, "How?"

I smiled tightly. "If I fell asleep at the wheel, it wasn't due to a lack of zees. I slept like a rock for a good eight hours the night before."

Sonia gave me the big eyes. "What are you saying?"

I narrowed my eyes. "I'm saying those drug tests are gonna come back positive. And when they do, it means Mariana Green slipped me a mickey. I'm saying it means she tried to kill me. Why? Because she killed Butch and I asked too many questions."

****

I followed Johnny into the service bay the next day after work. Other than all four tires having been removed, to my admittedly untrained eye, the car looked better than I expected. My favorite mechanic pointed to the chassis and then to the lump on my forehead. "All things considered, your car is in better shape than you, kiddo." He pulled a lever and the hydraulic lift lowered the car. He caressed the undercarriage as if it was a lover's cheek. "You're darn lucky this baby hit the berm. If she slammed into a tree at the speed she hit the berm at impact, she'd fold like an accordion with you inside and the momentum would have hurtled you over the cliff."

I cringed. "So, must I sell a kidney to get my baby out of hock?"

Johnny wiped an oil spot the size of a quarter from

the chassis with a rag. "Shocks and springs on all four wheels are shot, as well as the muffler and the front tires. The front end needs some work. Some scratches and dents to hammer out and re-paint." Johnny tapped the dented front fender and widened his eyes. "This could have been way, way worse. It's a miracle the car wasn't totaled."

I shuddered. "No structural damage? The frame is ok?"

He patted the undercarriage. "If the frame was bent, you'd have to junk the car. No way to fix it." He wiped his grease-stained hands on a towel and kindly cuffed my shoulder. "You pushed the envelope too far this time, Holly Swimsuit. Next time you might not be so lucky. Next time you might get yourself killed. Dead is forever. Do me a favor and watch yourself, will ya?" He grinned impishly, and two cute dimples cratered his cheeks. "Remember, I have two more kids to put through college." The hydraulic whooshed as he raised the rack back to the highest position and motioned for two waiting mechanics to finish the work on my car. "Come back tomorrow after you're done for the day. The car will be ready late afternoon."

Johnny's sharp laugh came out as a combination of bark and snort. "It'll be tough for you to manage, but try not to get into any more trouble between now and then."

Everyone in LA was a wannabe comedian.

Chapter Twenty

The unmistakable whir of the fax machine roused me from the quarterly sales report I'd been studying. Our showroom manager Patti brought the hospital lab report to my desk. I read it from top to bottom three times. The only things I understood were my name, the test date and time, and the words result: *positive*. My pulse roared in my ears.

I faxed the report to my resident expert for a translation. The receipt confirmation came through, so, I picked up the phone and dialed. An official-sounding voice answered on the third ring. "Good afternoon. Los Angeles County Medical Examiner's Office. Doctor Sophie Cutler speaking. You gun 'em, we gut 'em."

I laughed. "You missed your calling. You should give up performing autopsies and start performing your comedy routine in front of an audience."

Snip joked, "Angling to be my manager?"

I scoffed. "As if. You're unmanageable. But before you open in Vegas, I need to borrow your brain."

"For…?"

I rolled my eyes. "I sent you a fax."

Snip said, "I get a zillion faxes a day. When was it sent?"

I crossed my eyes. "Five freaking minutes ago."

She groaned. "If it's another set of jokes for the john, I've no time to read them now. Besides, you really should fax those kinds of things to my house and not at work. My boss was not amused."

I clucked my tongue. "Oh, come on, Doctor Death. Not this BS again. Geesh, you've got the memory of an elephant. It was *one* freaking time. *Two years ago*, for crying out loud. Get over it already, for heaven's sake. No jokes this time. I faxed you the lab test results from Cedars."

Snip asked, "What's it say?"

I flexed my fingers, imagining me strangling her through the phone. "Good grief, woman. If I *knew* what it said, I wouldn't need to ask you for an explanation."

She tsked. "Ok, don't twist your panties into square knots. Lemme see." She rustled a bunch of papers and said, "Ok, I see it. Gimme a minute to read the results." Sophie whistled loud as a longshoreman. "Holy moly. After what you ingested, you *should* be one of my patients."

My heart jumped to my throat. "Why? What was in the report?"

Snip clucked her tongue. "Considering your weight and height, you had enough Diazepam in your system to sink a whale."

I asked, "Which is?"

Snip said, "Diazepam is benzodiazepine."

I gritted my teeth. "English please."

Doctor Death replied. "It's a prescription medication prescribed for anti-anxiety. Better known to the world as Valium."

I asked, "How much was in my system?"

"Twenty milligrams."

The metric system and I are not BFFs. "And this is a lot?"

She said, "More than double the normally prescribed amount for an average adult. And remember, no one taking this medication takes the entire daily dosage at one time. Depending on the dosage, one pill is taken two to four times a day. You had twice as much in your system in a shorter time than a highly medicated anti-anxiety patient takes over a complete day. Two of the big side effects of Valium are dizziness and drowsiness, especially with higher dosages. No wonder you were unable to keep your eyes open and staggered around like a drunk. Driving should be avoided after taking this medication for five to seven hours. It's a miracle you weren't killed."

I spat. "Mariana Green tried her best to make it happen. Bet she's not doing the happy dance right now."

Snip asked, "Did you fax the report to Detective Jones?"

I said, "Not before finding out the meaning of the test result."

Snip said, "I'll fax it to him with an explanation, but don't expect him to do much with it."

I shook the phone receiver. There must be something wrong with the line. "Are you nuts? I *expect* him to arrest Mariana Green for attempted murder."

Once again Sophie Cutler was the messenger delivering more bad news. "With no proof Mrs. Green administrated the medication to you, her arrest is not gonna happen."

I levitated out of my chair. "Are you sniffing the formaldehyde? I was *alone* with Mariana Green in *her* house. She has a prescription bottle with *Valium* pills in her medicine chest. I wasn't drowsy until I drank the tea *Mariana Green* served me. Who else do you think

Susie Black

slipped me a mickey? Sigmund?" I snapped my fingers. "Wait a sec. I just remembered something to prove it. The tea she served this time tasted different than the first. The second brew didn't taste as bitter as the first, but I noticed a slight metallic aftertaste with this one. Does the difference in flavor mean anything?"

Snip said, "Yeah, it does. A metallic aftertaste is often associated with Valium."

Hallelujah. "Tada. Your proof on a silver platter."

Doctor Killjoy said, "Don't get too excited. Unless you can produce a sample of the exact Valium-laced tea in the same unwashed teacup you drank from on the day you visited her and prove Mrs. Green served it to you in that exact cup on the same day in her house, the only proof you have is you ingested a huge dose of Valium somewhere, sometime that day. You accuse her of attempted murder, and Ms. Green says you went into her bathroom, found the Valium, and were so distraught over Ms. Levine's arrest, you swallowed half the bottle of pills to end it all? Sorry pal, the most you have is one butt-ugly case of he said/she said."

I sent my resolve through the phone line so there was no question of my intentions. "If you think I'm gonna let her get away with this, you're kidding yourself. If Jones won't arrest her based on this, then I guess I'm gonna have to get a confession out of her myself."

Snip pleaded. "Don't do anything stupid. Stupid is the way people get killed."

As I've always said, no one ever confused me with Albert Einstein. Sometimes, stupid is my middle name.

Chapter Twenty-One

I swear Snip and the cops rehearsed their lines from the same script. "Ms. Schlivnik," the cop barely controlled himself. "Do you expect me to arrest Ms. Green for serving you tea?"

I squared my shoulders. If you want something done, do it yourself. Time to regroup and activate plan B. Which I would do, the moment I came up with it. Cripes. Who am I kidding? Color me fresh out of ideas.

The phone rang as I mentally wrote out the guestlist for my pity party. I picked up the receiver. Buddy LaValle was on the line. We hadn't spoken for a couple of days and it was more than a few since we'd seen one another. He'd been busy settling into his new job and house hunting, and I'd been busy trying not to get dead. I must be mighty depressed. For once, my heart didn't bang loud as a bass drum at the sound of his voice.

"Hey, Holly Swimsuit, it's Buddy from the other LA. I realize it's last minute, but I hope you and Sigmund are available to join me for dinner tonight at my new house. I'm all moved in, and I want y'all to be my first dinner guests."

In life, timing is important. Could his be any worse? Another complication I didn't need. All I wanted? My go-to pick-me-up combination: pizza, wine, ice cream, and my hound. I opened my yap to ask for a raincheck, but he stopped me dead in my tracks. "Don't feed

Sigmund beforehand. I have somethin' special for him. An jes' so ya know, I'm cookin' Mee-Maw's secret recipe jambalaya."

"Should I bring white wine or red?" Who says a girl can't be bought?

Santa Monica is famous for its pricey real estate, expansive ocean views, and the pier and infamous for a lack of residential street parking. I left work and raced back to the marina to fetch my pooch at the doggie day spa, with barely enough time left to buy the wine and find a parking spot on a street not closer to the marina than Buddy's bungalow five blocks east of the pier.

Naturally, with me in a hurry, the check-out line at Vinos del Mundo snaked to the back of the store. By the time I checked out and got back to the car, rush hour traffic on Lincoln was bumper to bumper. I checked my watch. We'd never make it to Buddy's house on time. I called to say we'd be late and then dialed Mariana Green's home number. I clicked open the recording app on the phone. Maybe I'd get lucky and she'd slip up. As if. She answered out of breath and said she was on her way out the door, but she'd be at her boat the next afternoon to hand over the keys to the new owner and for me to stop by then.

I hung up with Mariana and tapped the top of Siggie's head. "Holy guacamole, Sig. Good thing I called Mariana. Otherwise, we might never find the evidence we need to get Queenie out of jail."

Siggie perked up at the sound of his pal Queenie's name. He was no different from the rest of us. He missed her too. "Woof."

I gave him a love scratch behind his left ear. "The answer to this mystery isn't at Mariana's house. So, it has to be someplace on her boat. Guess you and me are going to say bon voyage to *By the Numbers* tomorrow, right?'

Siggie tilted his head to the side, thinking over his reply. He gave it a couple of beats then agreed. "Woof." Then he stuck his head out the window and lolled his tongue in the air.

The parking Goddess smiled at me and it only took two loops around the neighboring streets to find an available, legal spot. Siggie and I sprinted the two blocks north of Buddy's place and miraculously, we were only ten minutes late.

I rang the doorbell of his cerulean blue-painted circa fifties bungalow matching the color of the Pacific on a calm day. Buddy opened the door and his jaw dropped as he got a gander at my battered face. White as a sheet, his hand shook when I handed him the two bottles of wine as he ushered us in. Oops. My bad. In my excitement over the menu, I'd neglected to give him a heads up on my latest escapade.

He set the bottles on a glass-top rattan side table adjacent to the couch and folded me into his strong arms. His lips brushed my cheek and he whispered into my hair. "My goodness, girl, what the Sam Hill kind of mess did you get yourself into now?" He held me at arm's length and studied my wounded face. I finished telling the tale, and he shook his head in amazement. "Apparently, I cain't let you outta my sight for a minute."

I took a sniff, and the pungent aroma emanating from the kitchen made my mouth water. Buddy grinned and looked at his watch. "Ten minutes until chow time." He turned one-eighty around the house. "It's a small place. We got jes' enough time for the nickel tour."

Typical of the 1950's style, the layout of the bungalow was a series of small rooms. We started at the rear of the house with two bedrooms and a bath and worked our way back to the living room and kitchen. The master bedroom was tastefully done in masculine blues and grays. The second, smaller guest room was set up as an office. A handmade ragdoll constructed of fabric swatches sat on the desk next to a computer. The walls displayed a gallery of photos as a shrine to Buddy's late wife and child. The ghosts of Marie and Justine moved into the bungalow with Buddy. Sigh.

In addition to the side rattan table, the rectangular living room sported a black leather sofa and a glass and chrome-trimmed coffee table in front of it. A matching love seat sat on one side and a recliner on the other. A big-screen television faced the sofa. A gorgeous painting of a colorful bayou took up three-quarters of the wall behind the sofa. Buddy traced the artist's initials M LV and smiled. "Marie was quite an artist, wasn't she? I gave all her other paintings to her Mama when I sold our house, but I couldn't bear to give this one away. This is the bayou I grew up near." His voice cracked. "She painted it for my thirtieth birthday." My heart ached for Buddy and broke for the love apparently, never meant to be.

At the ding of the oven timer, I practically pole-vaulted to the cozy kitchen with its Formica counters, a linoleum-covered floor, and old-fashioned appliances. Since the kitchen was too small for two to work at the same time, I sat at the butcherblock table set for two and sipped my wine. I giggled as Buddy donned a chef's toque and an apron which declared in big red letters "CAJUN COOKS DO IT HOT & SPICY" He strutted the length of the narrow kitchen with the style and grace of a runway fashion model. He fingered the apron and bragged. "Don't you love the housewarmin' gift from Mee-Maw?"

Sigmund barked his approval…. or a reminder to Buddy that he was also invited to dinner and expected to be fed. Flip a coin. Buddy scratched Siggie under the chin. "Don't worry, my furry four-legged friend. I haven't forgotten you." Buddy took a takeaway box labeled *Doggie Delights, home of gourmet Canine Cuisine* out of the refrigerator, and spooned the contents into a ceramic bowl. He filled Siggie's travel water bowl and put it next to the food on a floor mat. Siggie stuck his big head into the bowl and never came up for air.

I widened my eyes. "Good grief, this is some gourmet delight. He attacked the food as though his last meal was a week ago." I crossed my heart. "You'd never tell by the way he's gobbling as if the Russians are in the hallway confiscating the food supply, but I swear, I do feed him every day, twice a day."

Buddy pointed to the bowl and laughed. "No worries. He doesn't look as if he's missed a meal. He's eating the Chef's special at Doggie Delights. Grilled chicken, sweet potatoes, squash, and spinach cooked in a secret sauce."

I groaned. "Fanfreakingtastic. Thanks a bunch. Now I'll never get him to settle for his regular dog food."

Buddy leaned across the counter. "Allow me. This ought to solve your problem." Buddy batted his eyes and handed me a menu I swatted away.

Siggie wolfed down the food in five huge gulps, belched twice, and made himself at home. He stretched out under the kitchen table and snored loud as a freight train five minutes later.

As advertised on Buddy's apron, the delicious jambalaya tasted hot and spicy. The conversation? Anything but.

Buddy observed me over his wineglass. "So, what's your game plan?"

As if. I needed another lecture like I needed a bigger tush. I smiled sweetly and batted my eyes. "Why do you think I have one?"

He gave me the stink eye. "I'm familiar with your looks. Might not be a good plan, but you've got one."

I grinned evilly and winked. "If I tell you I'd have to kill you."

He reached for the sky as though being mugged. "Then, in that case, would you desire coffee with dessert?"

Chapter Twenty-Two

An hour later we said our thanks for a lovely evening, wished Buddy good luck with the new house, and headed back to the barn. Siggie and I arrived at our basin, but an idea bubbled up in my brain as we neared the security gate. I pointed towards the mouth of the main channel. "Siggie, Mariana Green didn't slip me a mickey because she thought I needed a good night's sleep. I'm close to proving she murdered Butch, and she was desperate to shut me up. No smoking gun was at her house, so it must be on her boat. Time isn't on our side. She's turning the boat over to the new owner tomorrow afternoon. I have to search the boat before the new owner takes possession. If I don't find the proof on her boat that Mariana murdered Butch, I'm out of ideas. And our friend Queenie is toast. Tomorrow afternoon might be too late. We have to get on Mariana's boat tonight." I gave him a love pat behind the ears. "Don't worry. I've done this before on another boat. If it's the same setup as the last time, it'll be a piece of cake."

Siggie tilted his head to the side, trying to understand me. "Yeah," I said, "I burgled another boat." My dog gave me the big eyes. Geesh. "Don't give me the big eyes. I wasn't alone. Queenie partnered with me before your time. We were desperate to solve another murder and save Sonia Wilson from going to prison by finding the evidence to prove her innocence on Ronnie

Schwartzman's boat. And we found the evidence all in one neat package. Just not to convict Ronnie Schwartzman. Ok?"

He barked one sharp "Woof." And as though he now understood the urgency of the situation, Siggie strained on his leash to pull me along at a faster clip. We said good evening to the security guard making his rounds as we headed towards the other side of the marina.

I checked the time. 10:30. The guard leaves the security office to make his rounds at the top of the hour, every other hour during his shift. The guard shack is located on the lower level of the first of the three apartment buildings closest to Palawan Way bisecting the marina. If the guard doesn't make any stops, it takes him about an hour to walk the circumference of the marina. We encountered him about sixty-five percent of the way from his home base, so we had about thirty-five minutes to find the key and search the boat. It would be tight, but if I found the key quickly, and everything went smooth as clockwork, I should be able to do a thorough search.

As we raced to Mariana's boat I said, "Boaters are creatures of habit. We all keep a spare key hidden on board. Most boaters are the same as me and hide the extra key inside a deck cushion. Let's hope the Greens do too."

"Woof."

"Thanks for the vote of confidence."

We rounded the turn to the west side of the marina in record-breaking time. Siggie displayed no signs of exhaustion when we arrived at the Green's basin. As for me? My calves were on fire and I found it difficult to catch my breath. I don't care how badly I panted. I was not, repeat, not joining any sweaty, stinky gym. I opened the gate and we walked down the gangplank. We stopped at the *By the Numbers* slip, and my heart sank. With every light on the yacht turned on, *By the Numbers* was lit as brightly as the Christmas tree at Rockefeller Center. Mariana must be taking the rest of their stuff off the boat. Or my greatest fear. She was busy destroying the evidence and dumping it overboard.

In case Mariana had the sharp ears of a bat, I whispered. "Siggie, Mariana is on the boat. She came down to the marina after her meeting. Bet she's onboard to destroy all the evidence. It would look mighty squirrely to show up this late at night and"—I made quotation marks in the air—'want to chat.'" I'd never get a confession out of her nor an opportunity to search the boat with her following me around. Even if she let us on board, we'd need a distraction or something to keep her occupied while I searched, but for the life of me, I was drawing a blank. No point in trying. All we'll accomplish is raising her suspicions. I turned back to the gangplank. "Let's go home and get a good night's sleep. We have a big day ahead of us."

Hopefully, all the evidence wasn't already tossed into the channel by the time we got aboard *By the Numbers*.

****

Siggie's frantic, loud barking woke me with a start in the pitch dark. If this kept up any longer, he'd wake the whole dock. Or was I just dreaming? A glance into Siggie's empty basket across from my bed answered the question. My heart jackhammered in my chest with the strength of a piledriver.

I flipped the light switch next to the bed, but it just made a clicking sound. The face of the clock radio was dark. My watch said midnight. I shook my head to clear the cobwebs. Siggie never did anything this crazy before. Why would a power outage send him over the edge? Must be something more to it. I pulled the baseball bat out from under the bed. With only a sliver of moonlight as a beacon, I felt my way like a blind guy past the main salon. I pulled a flashlight from the tool drawer in the galley. A quick check of the doors and portholes said security wasn't breached. Thank heavens. So why was my dog going nuts? Siggie's ears lay plastered to the sides of his head. His fur stood on end as though he'd stuck a paw in a light socket. He stood rigidly at full attention and barked his head off in front of the forward door. I pulled him by the collar and shushed him from barking to a low growl in the back of his throat.

I cracked open the forward door and stuck my head out. I scoped a one-eighty around the dock. The streetlights were on, as well as the lights at the top of the gangplank. A half-dozen apartments were also lit. A single light shined inside a cabin cruiser two boats from mine. My boat seemed to be the only thing in the marina with no power.

This wasn't the first time I'd been the only one with no power. When I first bought the boat, I learned the hard way not to let the coffee maker, microwave oven, and television run at the same time or the circuits overloaded. But in the middle of the night with no appliances running or an electrical storm to cause a power outage? The blood froze in my veins. The answer wasn't *inside* the boat. I hoisted myself over the forward deck onto the dock with my heart in my throat.

A faint hint of smoke wafted from the breaker box and power outlet as I reached the end of the dock. I yanked the damaged plug out of the outlet and threw it in the water. I blasted the dock power outlet and breaker box with the fire extinguisher and pulled the other end of the power cord out of my boat power outlet. Eight minutes after my nine-one-one call, the cavalry arrived in force and all hell broke loose.

****

The psychedelic light shows of the emergency vehicles flashing strobe bubbles created an eerie specter as they bounced off the walls of the apartment buildings across from the marina. While the firemen examined the breaker box, two LA County deputy sheriffs kept my dock neighbors at a distance from my houseboat, now swathed with yellow crime scene tape.

After the deputy sheriffs arrived, Antonio, the security guard, called the dockmaster to bring her up to speed. Twenty minutes later, Dock Mistress Audrey Camarillo showed up at my slip to consult with me and the first responders.

A fireman squatted in front of the breaker box and electric outlet. "See this?" Siggie sidled over next to the fireman and the nosy parker hound rested his head on the guy's shoulder for a closer look. The fireman laughed and gave my curious canine a howdy-do scratch behind the ears.

The fireman pointed to the marine power cable connected from the outlet to my boat. The interior guts of the marine cable are covered by a protective rubber encasement. The cable was slit open, exposing the wiring inside mid-cable to the prongs of the tampered plug. Several strips of aluminum foil anchored in place by a fistful of pennies laid on the dock adjacent to the breaker box.

The fireman said, "Whoever did this is no amateur. They knew exactly what they were doing. If they hadn't been interrupted, they would've jammed the pennies in the breakers and wrapped the breakers with the aluminum foil. The breaker would've blown and ignited a fire. With the rubber-coated power cable serving as a connector, the fiberglass boat would've burned to a crisp in a matter of minutes." He stroked his gloved hand across Siggie's head. "It's a darned good thing Ms. Schlivnik's dog scared them off." He turned one-eighty around the basin. "With all the gasoline-powered motors, they came within a hair of blowing up the dock and burning this entire basin to ashes." The fireman shoved his helmet to the crown of his head and whistled through a gap in his front teeth. "Somebody wanted Ms. Schlivnik dead. They came mighty close to succeeding."

The Los Angeles Sheriff's Department detective turned to me. "Any idea who is responsible?"

I motioned to the gate above the gangplank. "That's a security gate. You need a key to get into the basins. Every tenant has a key to the gate and their key works on every gate in the marina. I'm not saying boaters don't let outsiders in, because we all do. But this time of night, I doubt if a boater is still out, and if someone was, they certainly wouldn't let a stranger in."

Audrey shrank back in horror. "You're saying one of *our tenants* is responsible?"

I nodded. "Yeah, and I've got a pretty good idea which one. She was aboard her boat last night."

Chapter Twenty-Three

Detective Wadkins asked a bazillion questions. Some I had answers to, but to many others, his guess was as good as mine. I finished giving my statement minutes before becoming the butt of the old joke "I was a young woman when the day began." After some industrial strength begging and pleading, Detective Wadkins generously gave me a whole five minutes to board my boat and pack a bag.

Siggie and I made our presence known at Snip's house at half-past four o'clock in the morning. I suffered no guilt for waking her. Snip is an extra early riser, so she'd be getting up not much later than our arrival. Snip brewed a pot of strong black coffee. She'd need something stronger once she read the police report. She smiled sardonically. "I should be flattered. You are bound and determined to become one of my patients."

I rolled my eyes. "Don't flatter yourself. Thank Detective Jones. If he'd get his head out of his ass and do his job right, none of this hot mess would happen."

Snip sucked in her cheeks. "I hate to be the bearer of more bad news, but you're not gonna be any happier with him when you show him this."

I snapped, "Is it gonna take Mariana *succeeding* before he finally arrests the right person?"

****

As Snip predicted, I left the Rampart Police Station

madder than a wet hen. Why did I even bother? As though doing me a gigantic favor, Detective Jones barely glanced at the police report. I asked when he'd be arresting Mariana. He shook his head and said if only based on this report, then never. I asked why the heck not and he said the *alleged* crime wasn't in his jurisdiction. Even if he thought the evidence sufficient, which he snidely added he doubted, it isn't his case.

His cavalier attitude so disgusted me, that I snatched the police report out of his hand and left without the courtesy of saying goodbye. I stomped down the hall and barged into Miguel's office. Hey, what's the point of having a police captain for a boyfriend if you can't take advantage and pull rank every once in a while? Wait. Who said boyfriend? A few Chinese dinners, a couple of movies, and some laughs watching the weirdos on the Venice boardwalk made him my boyfriend? Is he? Do I want him to be? And if the answer is yes, what about Buddy? Overnight, I went from no man in my life to too many men in my life. At the rate the attempts on my life piled up, I might not live long enough to answer those questions. I shook off the dilemma for another day.

Miguel turned a doubletake when I stormed into the room. My injuries started healing, but the remnants of a shiner and the lump on my forehead hadn't disappeared. Before I said a word, he came around the desk and took me in his arms. His voice cracked. "You might have been killed. Thank God you're ok."

I pulled out of his embrace and snapped, "No thanks to your crackerjack detective who seems incapable of arresting the right person. Is it gonna take Mariana Green succeeding before Jones gets it right?" I jabbed my index finger into his chest. "I've had three, count them *three*, attempts on my life. Who's responsible?" My voice dripped with sarcasm. "It must be the menace to society, Queenie Levine." I wagged my finger and sneered. "Oh, wait, it can't be her. Inspector Clouseau down the hall threw Queenie in jail. Don't you find it rather suspicious Queenie and I *were together* during the first attempt on my life and the last two occurred *after* she was arrested? I'm getting close to solving this one. Butch Oldham's murderer is doing everything possible to stop me." I was itching for a fight and baited him. "Too bad you and your bozo detective can't pull your heads out of your asses long enough to see you have the wrong woman in jail."

To his credit and my frustration, the consummate professional Miguel Martinez kept his cool and refused to take the bait. "The police work with facts, not emotion. And the *fact is*, absolutely *no* physical evidence ties Mariana Green to Mr. Oldham's murder. The *fact is*, all the physical evidence is tied to one suspect, and the suspect is the one Detective Jones arrested. Queenie Levine."

I narrowed my eyes. "Fine. Do you want evidence? Tell Detective Jones to meet me with a search warrant at Mariana Green's boat this afternoon. You'll get all the evidence you need."

Miguel's dark eyes turned hard as diamonds. "I'm warning you. Don't interfere with our case again."

No point in wasting any more time with him. My words fell on deaf ears. The only way this case gets solved is on my own. I squared my shoulders and turned on my heel. I stood beneath the doorjamb and defiantly jutted my jaw. "Since you're not gonna help me, stay out of my way. Arrest Mariana Green when I get you the evidence. If I'm wrong about her, arrest me."

Chapter Twenty-Four

I called David and brought him up to speed on the festivities of the night before. I crossed my fingers behind my back and said I wasn't up to coming into the office. A brief pang of guilt twisted my innards into sailor's knots when he expressed relief I wasn't hurt and said to take as much time as I needed.

I hung up with David and my growling stomach reminded me that the last time I'd eaten was dinner at Buddy's house. I treated myself to a burger, fries, and chocolate shake at Coast Burgers. Detective Wadkins called as I finished eating to tell me my boat, as well as the dock, passed inspection and my yacht was released. If the evidence wasn't on Mariana's boat, would I be safe going back onto mine? If it all goes as planned, no need for the question to be answered.

I fetched Siggie from doggie daycare and headed to my basin. A quick inspection of my boat, now it's showtime. I snapped the leash onto Siggie's collar and we made our way to Mariana's side of the marina.

I said, "We'll play it by ear, don't you think?"

"Woof."

"Right. Depending on whether she's alone or the new owner is aboard. If she's alone, it's gonna be tough to search the boat. If the new owner isn't aboard, you're gonna need to distract her."

"Woof, woof."

I gave him the stink eye. "How do I know? You're smart. Be creative. You'll think of something. Hopefully, the new owner is aboard and Mariana will be busy with him. Then you won't need to distract her. She'll be too busy to pay much attention to us."

"Woof."

We traversed the gangplank to Mariana's slip and I breathed a sigh of relief. Mariana and a casually dressed, clean-shaven, middle-aged man with brown hair and kind-looking gray eyes sat across from one another at her galley table. I rapped three times on the forward rail and raised my voice loud enough for them to hear. "Ahoy. Permission to board requested."

Mariana paled, but before she responded, the man flashed a hundred-thousand-watt smile and opened the fore doorway. "Permission to come aboard is granted." We climbed the three steps and crossed over the forward rail. He extended his right hand. "Hello. I'm Daniel Nelson." He pinwheeled one-eighty with his arms. "I bought *By the Numbers*. And you are?"

I said, "One of your neighbors, Holly Schlivnik. I live on a houseboat on the east side of the marina." I patted Siggie's head. "And this is Sigmund, but his friends all call him Siggie."

Daniel bent down and held out his hand. "Hello. Nice to meet you, Sigmund. I hope we'll be friends. May I call you Siggie?"

Siggie slid his paw over Daniel's palm and said, "Woof!"

Daniel threw his head back and laughed out loud. "Excellent. Then Siggie it is." I nodded my agreement when Daniel motioned to Mariana. "You must want to wish Mariana bon voyage?"

We crowded around the breakfast nook galley table. Mariana's eyes widened and she stuttered her stilted greeting. "I-It's nice s-seeing you. I-I'm a little -s-surprised. I-I didn't expect to s-see you again so, so, ah, s-soon."

Ha! I bet you are. Her discomfort made me smile. "Remember we talked last night? I said I wanted to ask you some questions and you said you couldn't speak then, but you'd be at the marina this afternoon. You invited me over, so I came."

Mariana patted her lips to disguise a yawn. "Gee, please excuse me. I got in late last night." She blinked guilelessly and laughed. "My weekly mahjong game broke up two hours later than usual. I didn't get home until well after ten-thirty."

My Aunt Fannie's tush. Good grief. The woman lied as smoothly as a campaigning politician. For once I controlled my tongue and managed to keep those thoughts to myself. I smiled sweetly. "I couldn't let you leave us without saying goodbye."

Mariana replied gamely. "No, I suppose not." She rattled the sheaf of papers. "Daniel and I are almost through signing the paperwork. When we finish signing the documents, a few things remain below that I need to show him how to work. We should be finished with everything in around fifteen minutes. Why don't you wait on the deck? After everything is done, we'll go over to the marina cantina for a drink and you can ask me those questions. Ok?"

A fierce gust of wind picked up and blew the forward door closed. Daniel said, "Mariana, it's awfully windy for Holly to wait for you on the deck. Better let her hang out in the main salon, ok?"

Fantastic. With a bit of luck and care, I could search the room while they finished the paperwork. Mariana shrugged her ok and Siggie and I went into the main salon. I angled myself to see and hear them but still look around. I tiptoed to the built-in wall unit and opened every drawer. Cleaned out. I unzipped every sofa and chair cushion and found a few quarters, but nothing else. I opened every desk drawer, and examined every shelf, even inside the two books on boating rules still left in the bookcase. Zippo-di- doo-da. If the evidence is still on the boat, it isn't in the main salon.

I'd no sooner completed my ill-begotten search when Daniel and Mariana came into the main salon and announced they were going below and would be back in fifteen minutes, twenty tops. The two disappeared down the narrow stairs and Siggie positioned himself as a sentinel at the mouth of the opening.

Twenty minutes to thoroughly search a boat this big is a push but doable. Fifteen minutes? Nearly impossible. The interior horseshoe design of *By the Numbers* is typical of most yachts its size. The focal point of the layout is the main salon, located mid-ship. All other rooms are adjacent to the main salon.

Since I'd already searched the main salon, I started in the galley and worked my way back to the two bedrooms and heads. The galley cabinets and pantry were empty as well as the refrigerator, oven, and microwave. Nothing between the breakfast nook cushions except stale breadcrumbs. I fired up the camera app on my phone and snapped pictures of the *By the Numbers* boat license with Dick and Mariana Green's signatures on it and the sale paperwork on the galley table. In the event I found any evidence, the date stamp on the paperwork and license helps prove I found it all the same day on Mariana's boat.

The two bedrooms and head separating them proved equally disappointing. Only one room left. The head between the main salon and galley. If it turned out to be a big nothing burger, I'd be up the creek without a paddle, since I had no way to search below. The medicine chest was empty as well as all the drawers. For giggles and squeaks, I checked the stall shower. Not even a bar of soap.

My heart sank. I'd done my best and got squat for my trouble. The only thing I accomplished? Piss off three cops enough to land me in jail. Hopefully, Ms. M. has a few tricks still up to her sleeve since I used all of mine.

Defeated, I turned to leave and spied a closet hidden behind the door. The closet angled narrow but deep. The shelves were empty but way in the back I spied something. I hit the cell flashlight app and shined the beam around. A Bainbridge Department Store shopping bag? Every room on the boat was picked clean and *one shopping bag* is in the back of the closet? Weird Mariana missed it. Well, it was in the back and no light, so I guess she didn't notice it. Or, I'd been right all along and she'd hidden the evidence, either planning to take it with her and destroy it, or frame the new owner instead.

Did I have enough time to check it out? My watch said five more minutes. I stretched my neck out the door of the head to make sure Mariana and Daniel weren't on the way up yet. Siggie still sat quietly guarding the top of the stairs. I heard no voices. If they came back now, how to explain myself? Impossible. But I'd gone this far, and Queenie's future hung in the balance. I couldn't let her down. In for a penny, in for a pound. I bent in half and crab-walked to the back of the narrow closet. Indeed, a Bainbridge Department Store shopping bag sat in the back. My hands shook as I pulled open the handles and my pulse ramped up to warp speed. Ding. Ding. Bingo. Bongo. Jackpot. We have a winner, ladies, and gentlemen. A large swath of jaggedly cut, blood-stained swimwear fabric lay stuffed into the bottom of the shopping bag. The pattern is the same print like the one picture framed around Butch's corpse on the cutting table.

I'd seen enough CSI TV programs to remember not to touch it with my bare hands, but I needed to see the stuff wrapped inside the fabric. I racked my brain for anything handy. Channeling MacGyver, in a flash, it came to me. I reached inside the zip compartment of my hobo and pulled out the tweezers and eyelash curler from my travel cosmetic kit. Time check. Three minutes. Crap. No time to wipe the rivulets of perspiration pouring down my face as if it was a Miami Beach July day.

I opened the stained fabric and my heart almost stopped. The whole enchilada was all gift-wrapped for the cops. Blood-stained men's boxer shorts, shoes, and socks. Blood-stained women's socks, tennis shoes, jeans, and a sweatshirt. Cellophane packaging from Flashy & Fun Lingerie in West Hollywood. A syringe with the remnants of some kind of liquid at the base. Eye pins that match the ones anchoring Butch's extremities to the cutting table. Bloody golf towel.

I hit the cell camera app and snapped two dozen photos. Something shiny caught my eye in the bottom of the bag. I angled the bag towards the floor and shook it. A roll of aluminum foil, half a roll of pennies, and a blood-stained Bainbridge Department Store credit card receipt with Mariana's signature fell out. I shot a half-dozen photos and shoved the stuff back in the bottom of the bag. I re-wrapped the bloody items in the swimwear fabric, put it on top, and closed the shopping bag.

Siggie let out three sharp barks followed by human voices. Daniel said, "Take it easy big fella. Where's your mommy?"

My heart jumped to my throat. I shoved the shopping bag back, crab-walked out, and closed the closet door. I yelled. "Daniel, I'm in the head." I tattered channeling a ditzy valley girl. "Little girl, little bladder. I'll be right out." I flushed the toilet and washed my hands for appearance's sake. I stowed the tweezers and eyelash curler in the cosmetic kit, put it back in the hobo bag, and walked out nonchalantly to the hallway.

I made a production of checking my watch and turned to Mariana. "I'm sorry, but I've gotta get going. While you guys were below, my boss called, and I have a major fire to put out. May I get a raincheck for tomorrow for our drink?" Mariana's dark eyes brightened with relief as she nodded yes.

With no time to spare, I almost jumped off the boat. Mariana might still dump the shopping bag into the channel. I'd taken this investigation as far as possible on my own. I needed help from someone with a badge and a gun. Now. I called Detective Jones, Miguel, and AJ. All three were either not taking my calls or miraculously out of the office at the same time. I emailed them the photos and left them each a voicemail that, even to my ears, bordered on frantic. The way things had been left with them, the chances I'd get a return call? Slimsky to nonesky.

I left a voicemail message for Snip and sent her the photos and prayed she'd be more successful getting a hold of the cops than me. But Snip is as bad as I am at checking voicemail. Her reply might come either too late or never.

Good thing I had one, as it was time to activate plan B. I made a U-turn and sprinted across the marina for the dockmaster's office. Hopefully, Mariana was still too busy with Daniel and didn't notice I went in the wrong direction to get to my boat. I flew past the dockmaster's assistant and headed straight for Audrey Camarillo's office. Her jaw dropped after I gave her the *Reader's Digest* version of the latest events. But she was reluctant to call the Harbor Patrol and LA County Sheriff's office. "This is an LAPD matter, not something the Harbor Patrol gets involved with and not the LA County Sheriff's jurisdiction."

Frustration crept into my tone. "Audrey, you're *dead wrong*. The harbor patrol gets involved if a crime has been committed in the marina. The marina is unincorporated and part of LA County. All our services are from the county including law enforcement. The sheriff's department *is* the police for the marina."

She wrung her hands as she paced the length of her office. "If LAPD doesn't think Ms. Green committed a crime, why will the sheriff?"

I opened the camera app and showed her the photos. If these weren't enough to convince her, nothing could. "I emailed these to LAPD, but they didn't respond yet. Say for the sake of argument, you're right about the sheriff not willing to get involved in an LAPD case. Forget about the murder and focus on the crime committed on this property instead." I pointed to the foil and the coins. "See those? Those items in Mariana's shopping bag are the same ones found by the cops next to my dock box, which is on the marina property. Mariana Green is the culprit."

Desperation amplified my voice to pleading. "Audrey, please. I'm begging you. It's gonna mean a lot more to the sheriff if the marina's dockmaster makes the request for help than one coming from me. We're running out of time. For crying out loud, make the call!"

Audrey re-examined the photos more closely and sighed. As the call rang, she pointed her index finger at the photos and growled. "You better be right about this. If not, Mariana Green is gonna sue the pants off the marina, and you can bet *your* sweet ass *my* sorry ass is gonna get fired."

And if I was wrong, *you* could bet *my* sweet ass was going to jail.

Chapter Twenty-Five

The Yentas sat transfixed as I related the tale the next morning. "Just imagine Daniel Nelson's reaction?" I slapped my cheeks. "The ink barely dried on the bill of sale and the next thing the poor guy knows, sirens are blaring, his newly purchased yacht is surrounded by the Harbor Patrol, a half-dozen LA County Sheriff's deputies rush aboard with their guns drawn, and Detective Wadkins serves Daniel the search warrant." I clasped my hands as though in prayer. "I led the detective to the linen closet and prayed Mariana's shopping bag was still in it. If it wasn't, I was toast."

Hope asked, "And?"

Joan smirked. "Well, it obviously was still there since she's sitting here telling the tale and not rotting in the jail cell next to Queenie."

I breathed a sigh of relief. "Thank heavens, yes. The detective's forensics team opened the bag and took everything out. Every item I photographed was still in the shopping bag."

Hope asked, "Mariana Green get arrested then?"

"She probably jumped overboard when the cop handed Daniel the search warrant." Joan laughed and made a motion with her arms like doing the doggie paddle. "If the tide carried her far enough, she may be on Catalina Island by now."

I shook my head. "No, not then."

Sonia pursed her lips. "For heaven's sake. How much more proof do they need? A blinking red light isn't enough?"

Joan spat. "A confession signed in blood."

I shook my head no. "Nothing quite so dramatic. The dockmaster reached the detective right away and I emailed him the photos, but by the time Wadkins got a judge at the Santa Monica court to issue a search warrant, Mariana had already left the marina."

Joan tapped her lip. "Begs the question why she left the shopping bag on the boat? Why not dump it in the channel or take it with her?"

Sonia asked, "You said she received twenty thousand dollars over the asking price, right?"

I nodded yes.

Hope said, "Maybe she was in such a hurry to take the money and run before the guy realized he'd grossly overpaid and changed his mind that she forgot it?"

Joan said, "Nah. My guess is she tried to frame the new owner."

Hope snapped her fingers. "Maybe they arrested the new owner? Joan's right. For all the police knew, the shopping bag was his."

I shook my head no. "Nope. I confirmed Daniel met me for the first time earlier the same afternoon. Wadkins questioned him about Butch, and Daniel didn't know Butch Oldham from Butch Cassidy, so he had no motive. Besides, the sales slip in the shopping bag with *Mariana's signature* on it matched the one on the boat bill of sale. So, the only crime Daniel committed is being in the wrong place at the wrong time."

Sonia said, "I say Mariana passed on taking the bag with her and chance getting caught with it."

Hope shook her head. "The best plan would have been to throw it into the channel."

Joan stroked her chin. "Maybe she planned to toss the bag in the water, but the new owner arrived earlier than she expected, and she couldn't get away from him long enough to dump it?"

Sonia turned to me. "You said Mariana wasn't arrested then. She escaped?"

I shook my head no. "She was arrested, but later. After Wadkins and Detective Jones conferred over the phone regarding the items in the shopping bag, Detective Jones issued a BOLO. I talked to Ms. M. late last night and found out Mariana was arrested at her house and the boat confiscated by the Harbor Patrol as a crime scene." I widened my eyes. "It appears Mariana tried to destroy the evidence…along with the boat. She removed the transom drain plug, and the boat started to slowly sink. I drove by the boat this morning. It was draped with yellow crime scene tape. Even though the Harbor Patrol filled the plug and prevented the boat from sinking, it still listed on the port side near the stern. A crying shame. Such a gorgeous vessel. *By the Numbers* isn't worth much now."

Imitating synchronized swimmers, the Yentas turned their heads in unison to Queenie's vacant seat as Joan pointed across the table. "Then if Mariana was arrested, why is the chair empty?"

I opened my mouth to answer, but a familiar voice beat me to the punch.

Queenie Levine, in all her glory, dressed to the nines, sky-high stilettos and all, strutted to the Yenta table and gave each of us a fierce hug. She patted the empty seat, planted her tush, and deadpanned. "Good to see you girls didn't replace me."

I gave her the stink eye. "Not yet, but the day is young."

Joan lasered Queenie with her patented kindergarten teacher look of disapproval over the rims of her eyeglasses. "So, what's the story, Miss Queen Bee? You got sprung outta jail and forgot how to dial a phone?"

Queenie had the grace to blush. "Yeah, well sorry to disappoint you, but my getting outta jail almost took an act of Congress. They arrested Mariana, but Detective Jones had a burr up his butt about the evidence against her being righteous. He refused to release me until he received it and it was analyzed."

She made a face as if she'd swallowed a lemon whole. "I'd still be wearing the tacky orange jumpsuit if Ms. M didn't raise a ruckus when the detective's case against me fell apart. All the tests came back negative late yesterday. My blood type wasn't a match to the blood at the crime scene, and the only place they found my fingerprints was smudged along with the real killer's on my sweater buttons. Other than my sweater, no physical evidence was found tying me to the crime scene. My DNA isn't on the cutting shears or the eye pins or Butch's corpse or his clothes. Jones and Ms. M. went round and round, and finally, around ten o'clock he agreed to let me go. The paperwork took a couple of hours. By the time I retrieved my belongings and Ms. M dropped me off at home, it was one in the morning."

Queenie surveyed the table and grinned. "And pardon me all to hell, ladies, for some stupid reason, I just wasn't in the mood for chatting. All I wanted was a hot shower and my own bed."

Joan waggled her fingers and smirked. "So, your

dialing finger still asleep this morning?"

Queenie rolled her eyes. "Funny. Not. I had a ton of things to do and considering I'd be seeing you here in a few hours anyway, no time for chit chat. I sprung the cats out of kitty camp and then grabbed the first appointment at the nail salon."

She wiggled her fingers. "I missed my mani and pedi appointment last week. No manicurist on duty at the jail. Imagine such a tragedy?" She surveyed the table and batted her eyes. "You expected me to make my big entrance *with naked nails*?"

She drank a glug of coffee and gave my face the once-over. "Nice shading on the shiner, but the lump on the forehead, not a good look. So, Ms. M said you'd burgled another boat. It's a wonder you weren't thrown into the cell next to mine." She narrowed her eyes. "You sure you weren't a cat burglar in another life?"

I swiped the back of my hand across my forehead. "Trust me, if the evidence wasn't on the boat, I *would be* in the cell next to yours." I jutted my chin. "By the way, not to nitpick, but accuracy is important. Not a burglary. Only an *attempted* burglary. I went to Mariana's boat the night before *intending* to search it. But she was on board, so the burglary never happened."

Queenie gave me the big eyes. "And the shopping bag with all the evidence, flew out of the closet yesterday and magically landed in your lap?"

I slapped the edge of the table. "Har-har, Ms. Smarty Pants. Nice to see you kept your rapier wit while in the slammer. Mariana was aboard the boat at the time. So, technically, not a burglary yesterday either." I twirled a ta-da with my hands. "I just toured the boat and we both got lucky."

She saluted me with her coffee cup. "Thank you for not giving up on me."

I grinned. "Not a chance. Siggie would never forgive me."

Queenie gave me a round of applause. "You've done it again, Nancy Drew. Notch another solved murder to your belt. Congratulations." She grinned. "And see? You managed to accomplish it all on your own with *no help* from me."

My eyes filled. "Siggie is a good sidekick, but it wasn't the same without you."

Chapter Twenty-Six

Three Days Later

David Workman had assembled the executives for yet another interminably long meeting. He was carrying on about bookings or more accurately, the lack of, for almost an hour. I held a computer report over my face to hide the stifled grin as Queenie Levine executed a yawn so wide, it threatened to crack her jaws.

David glared at Queenie and snapped, "I'm sorry. Are we keeping you awake, Ms. Levine?"

Queenie yawned again. "Hardly. You drone on much longer, and I'll be comatose."

She yelped when I kicked her under the table.

David asked when she anticipated receiving several store orders she'd sworn before her arrest that she would receive in a matter of days.

She shrugged. "I've no clue." She twisted a nonchalant flick of her wrist. "What do you expect me to do?" She waved a pen under David's nose. "I can't put the pen in their hands and force the buyers to write. We have one foot in the grave. We're not in a position of strength, so before you ask, there is *no point* in complaining to store management. Get over it, David, and accept the facts. If the orders aren't in by now, we're not getting them. The stores weren't willing to miss deliveries waiting to see if we survived. They gave our business to other suppliers." She threw her hands in the air. "You can't get blood from a stone."

Gary, our head designer, and I breathed a sigh of relief when the meeting finally ended. We quickly ushered Queenie out of David's office before she pissed him off enough that he fired her. We'd all worked for David long enough to realize the boss fired employees for less. Queenie had worked for him the longest, and she of all people knew David Workman was not someone you trifle with, especially now. He was under as much, if not more, pressure to perform as the rest of us.

After her stunt, it was a miracle David didn't kick Queenie's tush to the unemployment line. The guy had a notoriously short fuse. David's management style of screaming first and asking questions later took some getting used to.

He reprimanded Queenie with nothing more than an icy glare. For a guy with an infamously hair-trigger temper, he exhibited remarkable restraint. Maybe he understood Queenie took her frustration with the stores out on him. Or, more likely, he'd spun his mental Rolodex along with the rest of us and concluded no one else in the industry would be interested in taking Queenie's place on the Titanic of the swimwear industry. To our amazement and relief, Queenie whistled past the unemployment cemetery this time.

The meeting ended about a half hour before lunchtime, so I quickly hustled Queenie out of the building to cool off before she opened her yap again and got herself into even more hot water with the boss.

The hostess waved two menus and called my name. We took the last open two-top in the back of the deli. We concentrated on chowing down mixed with idle chit-chat. We finished our meal, paid the bill, and walked out to the parking lot. I made her promise to go back to the office and kiss David's ass. Yeah, right. Good luck. This was Queenie Levine. As if.

As we walked towards Queenie's car, a pickup truck was parked too closely next to her car on the passenger side. From the side, the truck was the same make and color as Diane Gentry's. I walked behind it for a closer look. The license plate wasn't Diane's vanity 2 TEAMS. I shrugged it off and walked back to the passenger side of Queenie's car. I carefully opened the door so as not to hit the truck and scratch it.

And then fingers of doubt tied my stomach in sailor's knots. Say Mariana was the killer, but was she capable of pulling this murder off all on her own? Not a chance. She needed help, but would Diane and Kelly be willing to participate? And if my latest scenario was right? Opportunity was certainly important, but it all came down to who hated Butch the most. Flashing lights shined on Kelly and Mariana. With all these theories colliding inside my head, my poor, addled brain might explode. But whichever candidate was the right one, I still needed proof. And the proof was only in one place.

I tugged on Queenie's wrist. "We've gotta go to Diane Gentry's house right now to check on something. It might be crazy or it might be the answer to all our questions. If I'm right, I know who the killer is."

Queenie looked at me as though I'd lost my mind. She might be right. "What the heck are you talking about? You *already know* who the killer is. The evidence you found got Mariana Green arrested for Butch's murder." Exasperation peppered by annoyance spiced her tone. "*Now* you're saying it's someone else?"

I shrugged. "It sounds crazy, but yeah. Remember I said we were in the right church but sitting in the wrong pew?"

Queenie nodded yes.

I said, "I'm right."

The thoughts pinged around my head like numbers in a slot machine, but I was no gambler. "I have to call Snip to make sure I'm not barking up the wrong tree." I waved towards the parking lot exit to move Queenie along. "Let's get going. I'll explain on the way."

Queenie's eyes searched mine for answers, but she asked no more questions. She knew better. Queenie cut off a bobtail truck loaded with produce and tail-gated two city buses going north on Santa Fe Avenue headed for the westbound Santa Monica freeway. She zig-zagged her way changing lanes and going around the usual wagon train of semis heading for the same interchange as us.

Vernon, the unincorporated city just east of downtown LA where the deli was located, had no houses or apartments. No one actually lived in the town. But Vernon had no shortage of factories, warehouses, slaughterhouses, railroad tracks, truck yards, and traffic jams.

We crossed the last set of railroad tracks, and Queenie accelerated up the freeway on-ramp. If not for the restraint of my seatbelt, I would have been thrown through the windshield as we screeched to a stop at the top. I craned my neck out the window looking for an accident. But other than too many cars in too few lanes, nothing visible created the backup. Logically, at that time of day, we should have been going against the traffic. But this was LA, so all bets are off. Three in the afternoon or three in the morning, it didn't matter. Interstate 10 was guaranteed to be bumper to bumper in both directions. Regrettably, there was no other way to get to Diane Gentry's house from East Los Angeles that wasn't going to Cleveland via Cairo.

A string of colorful expletives and the middle finger salute proved to be ineffective methods of persuasion when no one let Queenie merge in. If she didn't move over soon, we'd end up either in San Pedro or Pasadena. Both towns were in the opposite direction from Diane's home. Queenie cut off a semi and muscled her way onto the transition lane, then forced her car four lanes over into the fast lane. The fast lane. Ha! As if. Whoever named it wasn't from LA. At this rate, by the time we got to Diane's house, she might be in Timbuktu. I closed my eyes and said a prayer Queenie didn't make the emergency lane her personal expressway, even though, in my opinion, if ever there was an emergency, this was one.

I pulled out my cell and dialed Doctor Death. Hopefully, my favorite coroner wasn't elbow-deep in a corpse. I drummed my fingers on the armrest as the phone rang and rang. Patience had never been one of my strong suits. "Come on, come on, answer the damned phone already." After a dozen rings, there was still no answer. A glance at my watch explained why. "Crap, she's out to lunch. Screw it, I'm calling her cell. This can't wait."

For once, Snip picked up on the first ring. Thank God. "Hey, Holly. You just caught me getting into the car. Can I call you back after lunch? I'm meeting two friends from med school and I am running a little late."

No way. We had a killer to catch. I yelped into the

receiver. "Snip, *please* do me a favor and go back to your lab right now!" I took a few calming breaths to dispel any thoughts she had of me as a lunatic. "I have a hunch who the killer is. I need you to run the DNA from the crime scene through the system and see if it matches Kelly Oldham or Diane Gentry. A rumor went around the Mermaid factory saying Kelly had a drug problem a few years ago. Maybe she has a record? Diane served in the marines. Get her medical records from the Department of the Navy. Also, is it possible for a diabetic who once took insulin by injection is now able to take it by a pill?"

Snip sputtered like a leaky faucet. "K-Kelly O-Oldham? D-Diane G-Gentry? Why? All the evidence points to Mariana Green, exactly the way you said. After everything you went through to prove it, *now* you changed your mind?"

Pleading was not beneath me. "Please, Snip. I am begging you to trust me before it's too late. If I'm wrong, I swear I'll never ask you to do another thing for me."

She might have been right, but the honk of Sophie Cutler's unladylike snort got my Irish up. I growled deep in my throat, and she backed down. "Ok, ok. Calm your jets, Josephine. I'm on my way back now."

Hot diggity, now we'd get someplace. I dialed it back ten notches. "What about the insulin question?"

Snip replied, "Yes, it's common. If the patient's condition stabilizes or improves, they don't always need the insulin to get into the bloodstream as fast as via injection, so the physician could switch them to a tablet regimen. Why?"

I said, "The prescription we found in Diane's medicine chest is in tablet form, remember? I wanted to make sure if she took insulin via injection at one time, maybe she still has some syringes."

Snip said, "Ok, I'm back in the lab now. Where are you? I'll ring you back as soon as I get the answers."

As if. If she knew what I was up to, she'd birth a cow. I crossed my fingers behind my back. What was one more little white lie between friends? "Out on fabric appointments. I'm not in one place long enough for you to catch me. Call my cell ASAP once you get the information."

Sophie Cutler and I were friends for too long for me to get away with such a song and dance. In my mind, I visualized her eyebrows meeting her hairline as she sighed. "Don't do anything stupid, please. Stupid gets you killed."

I gave her my best imitation of *Mad Magazine*'s mascot Alfred E. Neuman. "Who, me?" I hung up before digging myself into a deeper hole.

Queenie cocked a brow. "Any reason not to tell Dr. Cutler where we're going?"

I crossed my fingers behind my back a second time. "I don't want to say anything until she gives us the answer. No sense looking idiotic unnecessarily."

The freeway finally opened up west of Crenshaw Blvd., and Queenie put the pedal to the metal to make up some time. Ten minutes later, we exited onto Overland Avenue and she gave me the big eyes. "Ok, let's not keep this revelation of yours a state secret any longer. Why am I driving to Diane Gentry's?"

I asked, "Do you remember Diane's vanity license plate?"

Queenie gave me a sideways glance. "No. Why?"

I rolled my eyes. "Don't you remember seeing it?"

Annoyance crept into my tone. "You parked right behind her truck the last time we went to her house."

Queenie shrugged. "Sorry. No clue."

Diane's quiet, tree-lined street is a half mile north of Overland. Mid-block, we pulled into her driveway. Diane's pickup truck sat parked tandem next to Kelly's sportscar. Queenie parked behind the truck. I pointed to the plate. "Look at the plate. It says 2 TEAMS. Do you get it now?"

She shrugged. "So, she roots for both the Angels and Dodgers? Who cares?"

The woman was so smart most of the time, but sometimes Queenie could be as thick as a brick. I took a breath and tried not to throttle her. I bit back the sarcasm and replied in a tone normally reserved for speaking to a slow-witted child. "She might, but that's not the meaning of the license plate."

I may as well be speaking Swedish. Queenie rolled her eyes and threw her arms in the air. "Then I have no freaking idea what the damned thing means. For crying out loud, quit playing twenty questions already and just tell me."

I shook my head sadly. "You are naïve, aren't you?" I pointed to the plate again. "Come on, Queenie, you aren't *that* dense. It means…"

Then my cell rang. "Hey, it's me." Snip announced herself without announcing herself. I put the phone on speaker so we could both hear. "No criminal record on Kelly Oldham. Her drug problem occurred as a minor, so her file is sealed. But you are right about Diane Gentry. She was a medic in the US Marines. How'd you find out?"

I said, "The letters SF are tattooed on her arm. They

stand for Semper Fi. Short for Semper Fidelis. Latin for Forever Faithful. That's the US Marine Corp motto."

Snip said, "I ran her DNA, and Diane Gentry is a perfect match to the DNA at the crime scene. No doubt about it, she's the killer. And before you ask, yes, I've already got a call in to Detective Jones." The synapses snapping in Sophie's brain crackled strong enough that when she made the connection, they came through the phone with the pulse of an electric current. "*Please* tell me you're not at Diane Gentry's house."

Before I could reply with a sarcastic wisecrack she wouldn't appreciate, someone reached around from behind and smacked the cell phone out of my hand with the butt of a pistol. The person stepped on the cell with the heel of a heavy work boot. The phone made a snap, crack, and pop sound as it disintegrated into a bazillion pieces. Hopefully, insurance covered this.

Chapter Twenty-Seven

I lost my balance and fell into Queenie when Diane shoved us together and jammed the cold barrel of the gun into the small of my back. "Well, Nancy Drew." Diane laughed evilly as she stepped in front of us and pointed the gun at my chest. "You're a lot smarter than you look." She waved the pistol at her truck. "You figured out the meaning of my license plate." Diane snorted. "Kelly thinks it means I root for both the Dodgers and the Angels."

I glowered at Queenie. Yeah, Kelly, get in the boat and row.

Diane pursed her lips with disdain. "You'd think the note I slipped into your mailbox would get you to back off. Anyone else takes the hint. But not you."

Diane waved the gun at Queenie. "I should really thank you. Your comments and threats about Butch were extremely helpful in framing you." She shrugged an apology. "Nothing personal against you, Queenie. You were just in the wrong place at the right time." She shook her head. "I don't get it. The syringe in your golf bag should have been enough to put you away. But when that failed to do the trick, man, I scrambled." She snorted derisively. "Let's talk about your golf bag. Are you kidding with the candy-cane-pink job? How much more Barbie-doll-goes-to-the-golf-course can you get?"

Queenie stiffened but stayed mum. Maybe fear

rendered her speechless. If so, it was a first. With a nasty gun pointed at us, it wouldn't be the best time for Queenie to make one of her usual smart-ass retorts. For once, the megaphone of the mart restrained herself. Maybe we'd live long enough to figure a way out of this mess.

Diane smirked. "Good thing I stole your sweater. Your precious baby nailed you to the wall. Pity about all the blood. Hope you don't mind the new color."

I grabbed Queenie by the arm as she lunged. The sweater meant the world to her, but it wasn't worth getting dead over.

Diane spoke in a conversational tone, as though telling a bedtime story. "I've gotta give my pal Mariana credit. She turned out to be a lot smarter than she seemed." Diane laughed and pointed the gun at me. "Unlike you, Miss Marple, good-guesser Mariana figured out I killed that bastard Oldham. Of course, with no proof, going to the cops was out. But even with proof, she'd never turn me in. Turns out, she was grateful I killed him." Diane laughed evilly. "But confronting me with her guess was her fatal mistake."

Keep her talking. As long as she's talking, she isn't shooting us dead.

I asked, "How?"

Diane threw out her chest. "I owned her then. It was an easy leap for the cops to make from cheerleader to co-conspirator. If I went down, so did she. But I had to confirm her loyalty in case she was a shill. So, I gave her a job to prove she and I were on the same team."

I parroted. "A job? What sort of job?"

Diane graced me with a hundred-thousand-watt grin. "A job to shut you up for good and stop you from asking all those questions and sticking your nose where it didn't belong." Diane spat. "But the clown failed to get the job done, and you're still mucking things up. But not for long."

Diane sighed as though the future of the planet was her responsibility. "If you want something done right, you've gotta do it yourself. I gave her one lousy thing to do, and she screwed it up. The braindead fool had to be punished for her incompetence. So, I set my backup plan into motion."

The epiphany exploded inside my head with the force of a lightning bolt. My knees went weak as the rest of the puzzle parts jumbled around in my head then the pieces fell neatly into place. In a moment of clarity, everything made perfect sense. And I could finally scratch the itch I hadn't been able to reach. The thoughts in my brain dinged as loud as the numbers on a Vegas slot machine. But would I live long enough to share them with the cops?

Diane pointed the gun at the house and barked. "Ok, you two, let's go. Your detecting days are over. Nice and slow." Diane pushed us towards the house. "We're gonna quietly walk into the house. No heroics or I'll shoot you where you stand." In case I needed convincing, she shoved the gun a little deeper between my shoulder blades. "Now move it."

I swept my eyes to the houses nearest Diane's. Maybe we'd luck out and some nosy neighbor watched the three of us dance the gun-totin' conga line and called the cops. As if. The street was so quiet, not even a bird chirped. Other than the pounding of my heart in my ears, the street was as silent as a cemetery. I shivered at the analogy and prayed it wasn't the portent of things to come.

Chapter Twenty-Eight

Kelly's eyes bugged at our panicked expressions as Queenie and I stumbled through the front door. "Queenie, Holly, why are you guys here? Is everything ok?"

Oh yeah, Kel, things are peachy. What about you?

Unless this was an Academy Award-winning acting performance, Kelly had no idea Diane murdered Butch. And her reaction once she found out? If she turned out to be thrilled, Queenie and I were screwed. If she reacted with horror, maybe she'd talk Diane out of killing us. As if. Diane was fine admitting everything only because we wouldn't be around to tell anyone else. Nana whispered inside my head, "God helps those who help themselves." As usual, my wise nana was right. If we wanted to live, we'd have to save ourselves.

I tried talking to Kelly with my eyes as I snapped my head several times towards Diane. But making big eyes and jerking my head as though I was having a seizure failed to make our situation any clearer to Butch's wife. Regrettably, Kelly only had eyes blinded by love for Diane.

"Diane, what the hell's going on?" Kelly squealed as loud as the tires on a getaway car at the sight of Diane holding a gun. "Diane, where'd you get a gun? And for crying out loud, why are you holding it on *them*?"

Diane laughed maniacally as she tapped my head

with the barrel of the gun. "Miss Nosy and her sidekick figured out I killed Butch. Now I need to take care of them."

The high pitch of Kelly's screech could have shattered a windowpane. "You what? Are you crazy?"

Diane puffed up as proud as a peacock and took a mock bow. "All for you, babe."

Kelly whimpered like a beaten dog. "Why? Tell me, why?"

Diane speared Kelly with a look of pity mixed with annoyance. "He'd renege on your agreement and you'd let him get away with it. You'd end up with nothing for all the crap he put you through." Kelly still wasn't getting it, so Diane softened her tone. "Don't you see? I had to protect you since you couldn't protect yourself."

Diane still trained the gun on Queenie and me, but she seemed distracted while explaining herself to Kelly. I surveyed the room for anything useful as a weapon. A heavy-looking marble obelisk on the end of the coffee table worked fine if I was equipped with the wingspan of a condor.

"Kel, I love you. But face it, babe." Diane laughed. "You're a wuss. He'd yell a little louder and you'd fold faster than a losing poker hand. Don't you see? It was up to me to save you from the monster."

Kelly pointed to Queenie and me. "And now what are you gonna do with these two?"

Diane grinned. "Piece of cake. I've got it all planned out. I kill these two. We bury them in the desert, and then you and I get lost in Mexico and live happily ever after."

I strained my ears. Was that the whine of sirens, or the desperation of wishful thinking messing with my head? If the cavalry was on its way, it'd be great if it arrived before Diane shot us dead.

Kelly spat her disgust. "You're insane. I hated Butch, but I never wanted him dead. I just wanted him out of my life."

Diane snorted a laugh. "This is why I love you, babe. Your innocence is so sweet. But you're such a weenie. You never stand up for yourself. You just don't get it, do you? My way is the *only way* he'd ever truly be out of your life."

Kelly just shook her head sadly.

Diane snarled. "You should be thanking me. I did the world a favor by ridding it of the son of a bitch."

Sweet music to my ears, the sirens blared louder. If I heard them, then Diane heard them too. In case she didn't, Kelly helpfully pointed them out. "Diane, do you hear those sirens? The cops are on the way. You'll never get away with this. Put down the gun, and let's get out while there's still time."

As though reading from the script rolling through my mind, Diane said her next predictable line. "Then I guess I've gotta hurry up then." Diane shoved me hard. "Move it you two. It's time for you to die."

I lost my balance and tripped over Queenie's stiletto heel as I fell. Evil radiated from Diane's eyes as she aimed the gun directly at my heart. She stood ready to blow me away. My wits and the element of surprise were my only weapons. Now or never. I came up using my haunches, powered up with my knees, and launched myself like a rocket. I head-butted Diane in the breadbasket with all my might. Diane fell backward and wheezed like an asthmatic walrus trying to draw a breath and dropped the gun. It bounced on the carpet and fell between Diane and Queenie, but it was too far for me to reach. Diane lunged for it, but Queenie kicked the gun away with the heel of her stiletto and it skittered across the carpet towards Kelly. Queenie went for the gun, but Diane stuck an arm out and grabbed Queenie by the ankle. Queenie fell to her knees, but Diane lay prone at an odd angle and didn't have enough leverage to bring Queenie completely down.

I rolled on top of Diane's chest and tried to pin her arms down with my knees, but she moved too fast for me. I saw stars as she caught my jaw squarely with a sharp uppercut of her right fist. I rolled off Diane and turned my head to the side and avoided her follow-up punch as it whizzed past my right ear. Diane rolled away from me and rose with the smooth grace of a leopard on the attack. She stomped on my right hand with her boot heel. A couple of bones cracked as she ground the heel into my knuckles, and I almost fainted from the excruciating pain.

Diane shoved me aside with her boot heel. Kelly picked up the gun as Diane made a quarter turn and viciously kicked Queenie in the ribs. The air whooshed out of Queenie's lungs like a deflated tire, and she dropped faster than the Times Square New Year's Eve ball.

Diane walked toward Kelly with her hand out. "Thanks, babe. That was quick-thinking, grabbing the gun." Diane waggled her fingers. "Ok, lemme have it and I'll take care of these two."

From the loud shriek of the sirens, the cops couldn't have been more than a minute away. Diane snapped her fingers and commanded, "Come on, Kelly! Give me the damned gun. We've gotta get going."

Three sets of jaws dropped when Kelly gripped the

handle with both hands and pointed the gun at her lover. "I'm not giving it back to you. I could never stay with you. You disgust me." Kelly waved the gun towards the front door. "We're not going anyplace. The cops will be here any minute. The only thing you're going to do is turn yourself in."

Diane screamed, "I did it for you!"

Kelly smiled sadly. "No, Diane. Like everything else, you only did it for yourself."

Diane lunged for the gun. "You're nothing but a dumb, ungrateful bimbo. You don't have the brains to come in outta the rain!"

Kelly dodged Diane with a deft toreador move and snorted a laugh. "Ironic, isn't it? Butch said the same thing."

Diane spat. "You deserve everything the bastard did to you."

"Whatever Butch did to me is a walk in the park compared to what you did to him." Kelly's eyes filled. "Anyone capable of that is a monster who should be put down like a rabid dog."

Kelly and Diane were too busy attacking one another to pay attention to Queenie and me. I gave Queenie the high sign, and we crawled toward the entrance and hid behind the fronds of a large artificial palm tree.

Diane rushed Kelly and let out a guttural scream from the back of her throat. Diane tackled Kelly and they fell to the floor, struggling for control of the gun. Diane was a lot stronger than Kelly and able to twist the gun barrel between them. Diane turned the gun around into Kelly's chest. Kelly reared back and drove her stiletto heel deep into Diane's upper thigh. Diane howled like a wounded coyote and fell forward into Kelly.

The explosion of the gunshot sounded more like a cannon. The back noise echoed around the house. The reverberations bounced off the living room walls. Kelly and Diane were so tangled together, that it was impossible to tell which one of them had been shot. The loud gunshot drowned out Kelly's scream as Diane collapsed in a pool of blood. A red fountain of blood spouted out of a large round hole in Diane's upper chest. Kelly looked at the gun as though she'd just discovered it in her hand. She dropped the Sig Sauer as though it was a branding iron and knelt to cradle Diane's crumpled body in her arms.

Chapter Twenty-Nine

The odd combination of antiseptic and the sweet scent of a floral bouquet filled my nose. Where the heck was I? Either in a hospital or someone sprayed the viewing room in the morgue with a floral scent room freshener to cover the stink of a corpse. With a supreme effort, I pried my eyes open to narrow slits and looked around. If not already prone, the explosion of pain in the front of my head when the lights blinded my vision would have put me down. My injuries hadn't seemed life-threatening, but since there wasn't a space in the place not filled with flowers, maybe I was wrong and this is a funeral home, not a hospital room?

I almost cried with relief at the tethered tubes sticking out of my arm and the beep of the monitors. Not a single part of my body was pain-free. Even my hair ached. Had a freight train run me over and I was too dumb to get out of the way? Since dead people supposedly didn't feel pain, despite the odds and all those flowers, apparently, I could still be counted amongst the living.

I slitted open my eyes, and Snip hovered over me like a mother hen. She shoved a thermometer under my tongue and tapped two fingers on my wrist to take my pulse. I shivered as she stuck the freezing stethoscope head between my boobs. She held my eyelids open and shined a flashlight at my pupils. She instructed me to say

"Ah" and stuck one of those nasty sticks you gag on down my throat. Satisfied I hadn't expired, she read my chart and smiled. "Despite your continued efforts to become one of my patients, by some inexplicable miracle, you've managed once again to defy the odds and survive."

I said, "I see you still have the warm and fuzzy patient bedside manner going for you, Doctor Death."

Snip retorted. "And if you don't want to *become* one of my patients, then you better stick to selling swimsuits. As a medical expert, my diagnosis is sleuthing is not good for your health."

It was hard enough to breathe, let alone talk, lying flat on my back. But I fought a losing battle to press the button to raise the hospital bed. My right forearm and wrist were encased in a heavy cast with three fingers splinted. My left hand throbbed from a painful needle stuck in a vein and taped onto an IV board as big as a catcher's mitt.

I said, "Cut the comedy routine. It only hurts when I laugh." Ha! My left eye, my jaw, my teeth, my cut lips, and my right hand all hurt but I'd live. Which is more than could be said for Diane Gentry.

When I didn't answer Snip's call, my favorite medical examiner put two and two together and called Detective Jones. Nobody's fool, Jones was accompanied by five cruisers carrying ten LAPD uniforms armed with enough firepower to take down a small army.

Josiah Jones drove up over the sidewalk and onto Diane Gentry's front lawn just as the shot rang out. The cops stormed the house with their guns drawn, ready to take out a battalion. Jones and the cops almost succeeded where Diane failed by practically scaring Queenie and me to death. With four women down on the ground and the shooting over, Jones and the uniforms went through the small house and quickly cleared it.

Snip followed the cops into Diane's house and found Kelly and Diane entwined and drenched in blood. Snip gently extricated Diane out of Kelly's arms and laid the wounded woman down on her back. Diane was shot in the chest by a high-powered gun at extremely close range. She had already lost a tremendous amount of blood by the time Snip arrived. Sophie worked on Diane for twenty minutes to no avail and then pronounced Diane dead. As the EMS zipped Diane's corpse into the black body bag and wheeled her out on the gurney, Queenie and I grabbed Kelly as she collapsed. Snip sedated Kelly and sent her to the hospital for observation.

Queenie and I performed our best imitations of a couple of superheroes or a couple of super idiots, take your pick, and poo-pooed the need for our trip to the emergency room. We crack medical experts determined since we were vertical and breathing, we were fine. Snip's predictable response to our self-diagnosis? She burst out laughing and flipped us the bird. Snip urged us to keep our day jobs and dispatched us to UCLA Medical Center Hospital. We were delivered in a couple of ambulances replete with screaming sirens and flashing lights. Ms. Melodramatic Levine always loved making a big entrance. But even for her, this over-the-top arrival beat anything she ever imagined.

As they wheeled us into the UCLA emergency room, Detective Jones told Sophie he needed to question us. Sophie made it clear to the big detective that his questions would be asked another time.

Turns out Queenie and I are much better at hawking

swimwear than diagnosing injuries. Diane went down, but she went down swinging. While Kelly suffered a couple of minor cuts and bruises, her serious wounds, while deep, were the emotional kind. Who knew how long it might take them to heal or if they ever would?

Diane reserved her most vicious physical blows for Queenie and me. According to the cute teenager who suspiciously resembled Doogie Houser's twin brother playing dress-up as an emergency doctor, I had a concussion, a doozy of a shiner with an eye swelled shut like a boxer's, a pair of a split and swollen lips, two loose teeth, and let's not leave out a broken right wrist, three broken fingers, and a crushed hand.

Queenie got away easier with only a couple of cracked ribs. The doc wrapped her midsection and told her to move as little as possible. Naturally, Queenie was a lot more upset about her cracked stiletto heel than her cracked ribs. No wonder. A pair of her sky-high designer stilettos probably cost more than her hospital stay.

Something important lingered in the back of my brain, just out of reach. What was it? Suddenly my brain unscrambled, and my heart leaped to my throat. Oh. My. God. Siggie! "Snip!" I squealed like a stuck pig. A hammer pounded inside my skull as I threw the covers off and tried to get out of bed. "Hand me my clothes. I've got to get out of here! Siggie's been home with no food for...OMG! I can't even imagine how long he's been waiting."

Snip put her hands on my shoulders and eased me back onto the bed. "You're not going anyplace. Lie still. Siggie is fine."

Was she sniffing the formaldehyde again? "Fine? How can you say that? My poor baby must be starving and crossing his legs by now."

She tsked. "Calm your jets, Josephine. The older neighbor of yours? Muriel, right?"

I blinked yes.

"She took care of him last night."

I asked, "Who told Muriel to get him?"

"AJ called the dockmaster, and she contacted your neighbor."

Thank heavens Muriel and I had exchanged keys to our boats.

Snip said, "Since you're gonna be out of commission a few days, AJ took Siggie to her house this morning."

I whimpered in my shame. "I am a horrible fur mom. I completely forgot about him. My mother raised three kids. She *never* forgot to feed us."

Snip rolled her eyes. "For crying out loud, cut yourself some slack. You've been a tad preoccupied. If your mom ever spent as much time as you do fighting off crazed killers, she might have forgotten to feed her kids too. Relax. Your boy is probably having the time of his life playing with Peso. Your only problem will be getting him to leave when you pick him up."

Chapter Thirty

With all the drugs they pumped into me, my memory ran kinda fuzzy. I vaguely remembered Snip leaving and promising to come back after her shift. David and Gary arrived together sometime, but I've no idea when. Did David say I finally came up with a good enough excuse for missing the next management meeting? As if. Must be the meds playing tricks with my head.

Uncle Barry was apparently in the room for hours. I hadn't noticed him until he snored loudly, having fallen asleep in the guest chair in the corner of the room. Thank goodness he called my parents in Miami. He convinced them my injuries were not life-threatening, and they didn't need to catch the next plane for LA. Thank God. Good grief. Mom hovering over me and Dad deciding whether to hug me or kill me himself? The thought alone made me dizzy. Merde.

I tested my progress by turning my head slightly and cheered not seeing double. I still ached from head to toe, but I'd improved. No more white-hot stars every time I moved more than a quarter of an inch. The blinds were opened halfway to diffused light outside. I'd lost track of time. Which day of the week either just began or just ended? I convinced Uncle Barry I wasn't dying any time soon and he ought to go home. Tomorrow was another day, whichever one it turned out to be. I chose not to share the thought with my uncle. Not if I wanted him to go home.

My uncle left and five minutes later, AJ and Detective Jones came in carrying two armfuls of bouquets way too elaborate for get-well gifts. So, they must be peace offerings. A combination of disappointment and relief tugged at my heartstrings when the third musketeer wasn't with them. Guess this was my answer to a future with Miguel Martinez. We'd never get past our differences. So, it was better to cut the tie now, before we ripped one another to shreds. Some relationships were just not meant to be.

The two cops couldn't find an empty spot to put the floral arrangements. If the pace of visitors continued, I'd either need a gardener to tend the flowers or a bigger room. Jones stayed near the door and bounced on the balls of his feet. AJ strode across the room and awkwardly shoved the bouquet of roses into my arms. She smiled shyly. "From Siggie and Peso. They send their love."

My eyes filled. "Thank you for taking care of my baby. You saved my bacon."

AJ dipped her head. "Friends do this kind of stuff for one another." She cleared her throat and checked her watch. "It's almost feeding time at the zoo. I'd better get going before the natives get restless. I'll be back tomorrow. Call me if you need anything." She glanced at the bouquet in my arms. "I'll stop at the nurse's station and ask them to bring in an extra cart for the flowers."

I squeezed her hand. "Thanks. Hug my baby for me."

AJ gently cuffed my shoulder and headed for the door. "Will do. By the way, congratulations. You scored a first-class shiner."

Detective Jones shifted the flowers in his arms and held the door open for AJ. Once she left, he gave me an expectant look but made no move to come any closer. Waiting for a written invitation? We stared at one another like gunslingers sizing up their opponents. After five minutes of this nonsense, I said, "Detective, whether this is this a social call or an official call to take my statement, I suggest you come closer. The nurses frown on shouting across the rooms. I promise not to bite."

Jones grinned. "I've seen you in action. Hopefully, the teeth marks won't show too much."

I opened my mouth and jiggled the two loose teeth. "I wouldn't be too concerned if I were you. Thanks to Diane Gentry, my bite isn't too sharp."

Jones cocked a brow. "*Inspector Clouseau*? Really?"

I tried to grin, but it hurt too much. "I call 'em as I see 'em."

He gave me the big eyes. "Nothing shy about you."

I spat. "Maybe next time you'll pull your head out of your ass and listen to a voice other than your own."

Jones laid the flowers on the foot of the bed and folded his big hands over his heart. "Perish the thought of a *next time*." He arranged his enormous frame into the chair next to the bed and gave me the once-over. "All kidding aside, you put up one helluva fight. How are you feeling?"

I smiled sardonically. "Probably better than I look."

He took a small tape recorder out of a messenger bag on his shoulder and held it out. "You sure you're up to doing this now? It's always best to get a witness's statement as close to the event as possible, while it's still fresh in their mind. But Sophie Cutler will serve my head on a platter if we do this before you're ready."

I said, "I doubt I'll *ever forget* a single detail, but since you're here, let's give it a whirl. I'll tell you if I need to stop."

Chapter Thirty-One

They say sleep is the best medicine, but an endless parade of visitors prevented the prescription from getting filled. After thanking me for my statement and wishing me a speedy recovery, no sooner had Jones departed, than Buddy LaValle walked in carrying a giant teddy bear dressed as a doctor. Buddy bussed my forehead with a feathery-soft kiss and tucked the teddy under the covers next to me. I fingered the stethoscope dangling from the bear's neck. "Now this is something you don't see anymore. A doctor who makes house calls."

Wishing I wore my Betty Boop jammies, I pulled the flimsy hospital gown tighter around me. Thank God the gown opening was in the back. I'd dreamed of being naked with Buddy, but this isn't the way I envisioned him seeing my body.

Buddy stood amused as I rearranged myself. He reached over and pulled the sheet and blanket past my shoulders to the top of my neck. He laughed out loud. "Do you remember the first night we shared a hotel room? It was the beginnin' of June in Savannah and at least ninety degrees outside. Took the air conditioner over an hour to cool off the room. I wore gym shorts and a tee shirt getting ready for bed. You came outta the bathroom wearin' a sweatsuit zipped up to your neck."

It hurt to laugh, but there was no controlling it. I recalled the incident and blushed crimson from my neck to my scalp. Guess I hadn't progressed too far when it came to Buddy LaValle. Buddy's chocolate brown eyes found mine. But he looked away as his eyes filled. He brushed an imaginary errant lock of hair out of my eyes for something to do with his hands. His voice cracked. "I don't know what I'd do if I lost you. I've been frantic. I couldn't bear it a second time."

The question I fear I'd never have the answer to? Was it unbearable losing *me* twice or losing a *second woman* a second time? His touch still set my every nerve ending on fire, but would I be willing to share him with a ghost?

My game of mental ping-pong was interrupted by a knock on the door. Miguel Martinez poked his head through the doorjamb. His obsidian eyes locked with Buddy's and the captain asked, "Is this a good time?" Without waiting for an answer, Miguel strode across the room with an armful of the largest bouquet of daisies imaginable.

Enough testosterone filled the atmosphere in the room to cut with a knife. The two bucks sized one another up as though preparing to fight over a doe. Buddy stationed himself on the left side of the bed with his arm territorially draped around my shoulder. Miguel stood on the right side and laid the bouquet of daisies in my arms. He glared at Buddy and then turned to me. "Since daisies are your *favorite* flower, I bought every bloom at the flower mart." Southern gentleman Buddy LaValle responded by rolling his eyes. Meow. So, women weren't the only ones who lowered themselves into catfights. Holy guacamole. My love life just became a whole lot more interesting.

Miguel grasped Buddy's right hand when he thrust

it across the bed as I made the introductions. "Buddy, say hi to Miguel Martinez. Miguel, this is Buddy LaValle." They nodded their acknowledgment to one another, but neither one said a word. So, I babbled on to fill the awkward silence. "I've told you so much about one another, it's as if you've already met. Nice you two finally got the chance to meet in person."

Right. An introduction as warm and friendly as Alexander Hamilton meeting Aaron Burr. I gave them both the stink eye, and they gamely mumbled a stilted greeting neither meant a word of. Thank heavens only one of them came armed, or there might have been a shoot-out. Just one man was a lot of work. Two men were exhausting. Sigmund might be the only male I need in my life.

Buddy smiled at me and said, "I'm leavin' early tomorrow morning for the Big Easy to clean up some final things. I'll be gone 'bout four or five days, dependin' on how fast I get things done." His eyes clouded as his fingers grazed my shoulder. "But I'll rearrange my trip if you need me to stay in town."

I said, "No worries, don't change your plans for me." Miguel perked up after I said, "I have a legion of volunteer nurses to take care of me."

Buddy grinned and pointed to the IV drip. "Good thing I'm not dependin' on you for a ride to the airport." He wiggled his brows and demonstrated his Arnold Schwarzenegger imitation. "Ah'll be back." If Arnold's accent was more Daisy Duke's daddy and less Colonel Klink, Buddy's imitation would be spot on. Buddy lifted the stethoscope and spoke into it like a microphone. "While I'm gone, take good care of her." Buddy kissed my cheek, nodded curtly to Miguel, and waved goodbye as he walked out.

Miguel took the bouquet out of my arms and motioned to the door. "Maybe I should go ask the nurse for something to put these in? They'll last a lot longer in water." Concerned about the flowers or need an excuse to escape? Miguel made a face like he needed to fart when I motioned my head to the phone. "Nurse's station is extension 326." Nice try, Mickey. A volunteer brought a large vase filled with water and arranged the flowers in it. She put them on the table holding the other arrangements and asked if I needed anything else. I said no, and she wished me a speedy recovery as she walked out of the room.

Miguel squirmed in the chair next to the bed, unable to find a place for himself. He fidgeted with his tie and spoke to the teddy bear instead of me. "So, how are you doing?"

I put my hand behind the teddy's back and made the bear speak into the stethoscope. "The prognosis for the patient is good." The grin died on his lips when I asked, "Why did you bother coming? You don't want to be here. I'm in no mood for twenty questions or one of your lectures, but if you have something to say, spit it out already. If not, I'm exhausted, so, just show yourself out."

The words stuck in his throat as he choked them out. "W-why do you think? I-I been frantic at the thought of losing you." He fingered the stethoscope and said, "Looks as if I already did."

I pressed my unbandaged fingers together and played an imaginary violin. "Don't go down that road. Buddy LaValle isn't the one responsible for our problem. If you want someone to blame, take a long look in the mirror. If you were so *frantic* about losing me, you'd have listened to me and been there when I asked for help, but you weren't. The solution to our issue is simple." I held out my hand attached to the IV board as he opened his mouth to protest. "You want me to quit interfering? Arrest the right suspects."

Two men frantic *over the thought of losing me*? Guess neither one got the memo. You can't lose what you don't have.

Chapter Thirty-Two

Hard to believe it was only a week since the shooting. In some ways, it seemed a lifetime ago, in others only a moment before. By the end of the week, the swelling of my lips was down considerably. Puckering was still out of the question, but I could smile and eat without re-splitting my lips. The black shiner haloed around my eye socket had faded into a purplish-green, so I looked less a prizefighter on the wrong end of a right hook and more a psychedelic raccoon with a spastic wink.

My broken right wrist itched inside the cast. It was supposed to be good news. A sign the injury was on the mend. I met Snip for dinner, and she smacked my left wrist as I stuck a butter knife into the cast and scraped it across my right hand to my wrist. "For crying out loud, quit scratching, or you'll get an infection and end up losing your hand." Fortunately, I was a southpaw. I only used my right hand to wear my watch and balance out my purse and briefcase. So, now I wore my watch on my left wrist and kept checking the time on my right. A lifetime of habits was a lot more difficult to turn off than a faucet.

****

A look in the mirror confirmed the nightmare happened, and it happened to *me*. Yet, in telling the tale, it sounded as though I was relating the nightmare of somebody else's bad dream. My physical wounds healed faster than the emotional ones trapped in my memory and were impossible to forget. No salves existed to heal those injuries, no bandages adequate enough to cover those wounds. No way to silence the explosion of the gunshot, or the anguish of Kelly's scream still reverberating inside my head. I found it impossible to close my eyes and not see Diane's astonished face the moment the bullet punctured her lung and ricocheted to her heart. Every trauma expert said don't keep everything bottled up inside. They said that getting it all out is the only way to heal. Fortunately, I met with the perfect group of listeners every morning for coffee.

****

The latest copy of the *West Coast Apparel News* lay spread out across the Yentas' table in the mart lobby location of a Jolt of Java. The front-page boldface headline above the fold screamed *"Super Sleuth Schlivnik Solves Slaying!"* The Yentas saluted me with their coffee cups. Sonia scooped the newspaper off the table and waved it back and forth like a black and white checkered victory flag at the finish line of a car race. "Congratulations, *Triple S*, you've done it again."

I parroted. "Triple S?"

Sonia laid the paper in front of me and tapped the headline with a teaspoon. "See? *Super Sleuth Schlivnik.* Triple S. That's you."

The Yentas' jaws dropped as I shook my head and replied, "Yeah, but I am such a moron."

Normally a source of annoying distraction, I found the familiar din of the crowded coffee shop comforting as I gulped a fortifying glug of java before continuing the telling of the tale. "While I stumbled and bumbled my way around and wasted time fingering the wrong suspect, the killer's identity lurked everyplace I looked. When Diane worked at Mermaid, she parked next to me. I walked past her truck every day, and the answers were on it plain as the nose on my face: 2 TEAMS license plates and a USMC decal on the back bumper. And if I managed to miss the clues blinking bright as a beacon on the truck, they were tattooed on Diane Gentry's arms the whole time. I was just too stupid or blind to realize the significance."

Hope made a sour face and shrugged. "So, she rooted for both the Angels and the Dodgers, and she preferred men in uniform. Big freakin' deal. So, do I. Doesn't make me a killer, does it? You wanna tell me how *those* are clues to the killer?"

I surveyed the rest of the table. Nothing but blank stares. I restrained myself from rolling my eyes. A little slow on the uptake this morning, ladies. Maybe they needed stronger coffee or a second cup chaser? I waited a couple of beats in case the light bulb blinked on inside one of their heads. Dead silence. It might take all day for their epiphany to happen. So, I gave up and threw in the towel. "Ok, the significance is TT: 2 TEAMS. It has nothing to do with athletics. It means Diane was bisexual. She is who Butch had sex with before he died. SF on the other arm: Semper Fi is the motto of the US Marines. Diane was a marine medic. That's how she knew which drug to use. First Diane set Queenie up—"

Sonia interrupted with a waggle of fingers. She turned to Queenie. "Why you? Why not David? His was one helluva motive. It's a wonder he *didn't* murder Butch."

Queenie made a take-it-away gesture to me.

"No question about it. David was pissed, and with good reason. But David has always been more about money than position. He got a bucket of bucks, the job he loves with no strings attached, no corporate responsibilities, or liabilities if things went south. David accomplished what my dad always advised me to do. Don't get mad, get even. Butch stole David's job, but David got the better end of the deal."

When I finished, Queenie added her fifty cents. "Why me? For one thing, Diane and I go way back. She worked at Royal Swimwear at the same time as me. So, she knew about my affair with Butch. Everyone knew I hated the man. And it wasn't a state secret I swore I'd make Butch pay for destroying Mermaid." Queenie laughed. "I might as well have waved a red flag and said, *pick me, pick me!*" She pursed her lips into a funnel. "I handed her everything she needed on a silver platter to set me up."

I said, "Then after Mariana figured out Diane murdered Butch, she confronted Diane. Mariana hated Butch for destroying Dick and told Diane so. Big mistake."

Hope dipped her head. "Why? Wasn't Diane happy to have an ally?"

I smiled. "Oh, Yessiree. Believe me, she was. She had another easy patsy. Diane told Mariana to shut me up for good. But after Mariana failed, Diane punished her by framing her for Butch's murder. And she used me, her next unwitting stooge, to do her dirty work. Diane made a duplicate key to *By the Numbers* the day she and Kelly helped Mariana pack the boat up. Diane, not Mariana, was on the boat the night before I found the shopping bag. Diane, not Mariana, stashed the shopping bag in the closet. Diane planted the evidence in the shopping bag pointing to Mariana for me to find. Diane, not Mariana, tampered with my houseboat. Diane, not Mariana, rigged *By the Numbers* to sink."

Sonia tilted her head. "Why would she sink the boat? She planned to murder Mariana too?"

I said, "No. Diane rigged the boat to sink slowly, so she had no idea if Mariana would still be on board when it finally sank. My guess? Sinking it was a backup plan to destroy the evidence in case I missed finding the shopping bag. My dial stayed stuck on Mariana, but Diane proved to be the puppeteer pulling the strings all along." I hung my head. "I turned out to be as blind as Detective Jones."

Joan crossed her arms over her chest. "BS. Who solved the murder? You or him?"

Sonia waved an index finger. "And don't forget. Mariana *is* still guilty of a crime."

I dipped my head. "True. She swore she didn't kill Butch, but confessed to drugging me. She's been charged with attempted murder. She's gonna do some serious time. And unlike her husband, it won't be in a cushy club Fed. She'll do her time in a tough women's state prison populated by gang members and career criminals who'd cut her heart out for an extra piece of bread or just for something to do."

Joan narrowed her eyes. "So, you're saying Butch's wife wasn't his killer? Pretty hard to believe. The spouse is usually the murderer."

I said, "Initially she was the chief suspect, but it turned out Kelly had no motive. She and Butch signed a prenup. He left everything to his kids from his first marriage. I ran into Kelly while she was looking for

Butch at the factory the day of his murder. She was there to finalize their divorce settlement." I grinned. "You can't negotiate with a corpse, so he was worth a lot more to her alive than dead. Even though she cheated on Butch with Diane, Kelly still had a moral compass. She wanted Butch out of her life, but she never wanted him killed. Kelly had no idea Diane murdered Butch until Diane told her. Horrified, Kelly told Diane to turn herself in. Diane never clued Kelly into her plan. Why? My guess is on some level, Diane knew Kelly wouldn't go along with it. She turned out to be right as rain."

Hope scratched her head. "If Kelly didn't want her husband murdered, why did Diane do it?"

I shrugged. "She said she was protecting Kelly from an abusive bully who would renege on any divorce settlement. At the end of the day, given her issues with Butch, Diane hated him more than Kelly. Even as she drew her last breath, Diane had no remorse."

Sonia asked, "So, how'd she do it?"

"She arrived at the factory ahead of Kelly and followed Butch into the warehouse. Since Kelly had dumped him for Diane, I bet he wasn't too excited to see her. But she knew exactly which buttons to push. She played on his little man insecurities and seduced Butch into a false sense of security." I pinched my lips and made a sour face, as though I'd eaten a grapefruit whole. "While Butch got hot and bothered and not paying attention, Diane injected him with a paralytic muscle relaxer."

Sonia asked, "The same as the medication you take after a rigorous workout?"

I shook my head. "Nope. Dr. Cutler identified the one injected into Butch as rocuronium bromide. It's a drug used in conjunction with anesthesia during surgery to keep patients from moving during the procedure. This stuff is no *cure* for sore muscles. Once she shot him up, he couldn't *move* a muscle. The guy became paralyzed from head to toe."

Hope asked, "But how did she even know which drug to use, much less the way to get her hands on such a lethal muscle relaxer?"

I said, "As a marine medic with combat experience, Diane was familiar with the paralytic drugs used in surgery. She was diabetic and got all her meds on base at the commissary pharmacy. So, she was there regularly and knew the pharmacists and techs. She bought the syringe, and no one gave it a second thought. Dr. Cutler contacted the head pharmacist and found out several drugs, including rocuronium bromide, were stolen from the base. If Diane herself was unable to get into the area where the drug is kept, she probably bribed a tech to steal it for her."

Hope flinched. "Butch saw Diane murdering him but was unable to move and get away?"

I shuddered. "Precisely. He helplessly watched her murder him. He couldn't scream or move. It was the worst kind of death imaginable. He suffered tremendously before he died."

Queenie smiled evilly. "Oh, not completely. Let's not forget he got laid one last time." Queenie cackled. "If I know Butch, his performance prowess is the thing Mr. Macho probably focused on as he slipped over to the other side."

Chapter Thirty-Three

Being back in my office proved to be a therapeutic blessing. Putting out fires and solving customer crises brought a measure of normalcy back into my chaotic life. We took it as a good sign Queenie and I managed to get through the week without a relapse or dodging any bullets. To celebrate, Queenie and I invited the executives and key department heads to lunch. Mr. Smythe was also invited, but he begged off. He said this celebration was for members of the Mermaid family, and he was only the hired help. Mr. Smythe was a real class act though. He gave us our privacy but insisted on springing for the lunch.

While Queenie and I were in the hospital, the bankruptcy court accepted our offer. Queenie, Gary, and I met with Mr. Smythe before we joined the others for lunch to sign the final papers. I tingled with nervous excitement as I scribbled my signature a few bazillion times. I almost burst with the anticipation of making our big announcement, and the luncheon was the perfect venue.

With such a special occasion, we reserved a banquet table at one of my favorite eateries. El Caboose Rojo was a super cool restaurant inside a series of three old passenger train cars. The trio sat in a triangle on the west side of Santa Fe Avenue, adjacent to one of the many sets of railroad tracks encircling the area. An older guy dressed in a conductor's uniform replete with a fobbed pocket watch greeted us at the platform serving as the restaurant's entrance. He led us to our table in the main "dining" car and handed out menus designed as train schedules.

Despite it being a workday, no one complained when David ordered a couple of bottles of wine. David stood and tipped his wineglass at Queenie and me. Considering our brush with death, he made the most appropriate toast. "L'chaim," he said, and the group chorused back, "L'chaim, to life." No one knew more than Queenie and me how great it was to be alive.

I gazed fondly at my nine-to-five family. "Well, I guess we're the poster children of my nana's favorite expression: nothing ever turns out the way you think it will."

Queenie grinned as wide as a tunnel entrance. "No kidding. No one makes this stuff up. Considering how close she and Butch were, Diane is the *last person* I ever thought to kill him."

Our head patternmaker, Bernice Price mused. "With most murders, it usually *is* those closest to the victim who has done the deed."

David slapped his cheeks. "The story gets more bizarre, believe it or not."

Imitating a Greek chorus, we replied in unison. "How?"

Like fans following a tennis match, we turned our heads in the opposite direction when Ike took the baton from David. "Diane missed her calling. She should have been an actress. It turns out, she hated Butch for a long time." Ike slapped the table and laughed out loud. "Ironically, Diane was the friend of Butch's first wife before she knew Butch. That's how Butch met her. Diane disapproved of the heartless way Butch dumped his first wife for Kelly."

Huh? No-nonsense, just-give-me-the-facts production manager Ike Loach was not exactly the first guy who'd come to mind as a gossip. The company has a plethora of candidates. Harriet, Queenie, David, and Gary were my top four picks, hands down. Ike was a rank amateur compared to those professional Yentas. As though he read my mind, Ike put his hands out in supplication. "Through the contractor rumor pipeline, I found out *our Diane*, unbeknownst to Butch, was sent to Mermaid as a plant, a ringer, an industrial spy. She apparently was working for Stan Herman at Pagoda Swimwear for a long time."

David jumped back in. "We were always friendly competitors with Pagoda. Come to find out Stan tangled plenty with Butch over the years and was determined to get payback. After Stan heard Butch was at Mermaid, he and Diane compared notes, discovered their mutual hatred of Butch, and cooked up a scheme to ruin him."

Queenie turned to David and Ike. "Any idea what Butch did to Stan?"

The light of recognition shined in Gary's eyes. "I bet I do. Pagoda was on a real tear and cut deeply into Royal Swimwear's business. After Butch took over as the head of Royal, he stole Stan's head designer. Pagoda took a nosedive and never fully recovered."

The lightbulb in Queenie's head turned on. "Let me take a wild guess." Queenie cuffed Gary's shoulder. "The head designer Butch stole from Stan is you."

Gary clapped his hands and laughed. "Ding, ding, we have a winner ladies and gentlemen. Give the young lady a cigar. Yep, you guessed it right. I am the designer Butch stole from Stan."

Queenie's jaw dropped. "Are you saying Stan sent Diane to Mermaid to steal *you* back?"

Before Gary answered, David interceded. "Stealing him back was part of the plan, but not the main objective. Getting Gary back to Pagoda was the icing on the cake. But the real goal was to disrupt our production and destroy our reputation in the market for a great fitting product. They intended to ruin Butch by destroying Mermaid from the inside under his watch."

Queenie snorted. "Too bad Stan and Diane never counted on Butch being their biggest competition in the destroy Mermaid derby."

Straight as an arrow Ike wryly observed, "They might have succeeded if '*love*' didn't interfere. Their plan to ruin Butch was inadvertently foiled once Diane's affair with Kelly was discovered. Diane resigned rather than face the prospect of Butch discovering the affair." Ike's big body shook with laughter from head to toe. "How's this for irony? To cover her tracks, she told Butch she resigned to save him and not be the reason he failed to turn the company around."

Queenie's eyes twinkled evilly. "Must have been an Academy Award performance." Queenie sucked in her cheeks. "Of course, look at the audience she played to. Butch probably bought it hook, line, and sinker." Queenie squared her shoulders. "What goes around comes around. And those two certainly got theirs."

After the wait staff cleared the dregs of the meal, David stood behind his chair and smiled as if he had a secret. "In the spirit of 'if you don't go forward you go backward,' I have something important to discuss with you regarding our future together as the Mermaid team."

Three heads snapped to attention as my partners and I conferred with our eyes. I clenched my fists to my sides so I didn't deck the arrogant jerk. The nerve of this man. How dare he steal our thunder. This was not his announcement to make.

The bigger question was how had David found out? After Mr. Smythe's stern admonishment to zip our lips until the deal was signed, no way he'd be the one to spill the beans. Would he? We didn't breathe a word to anyone about the buyout except to our families. Certainly to no one at Mermaid. Even if Mr. Smythe prepped David out of respect, would *David Workman* have taken the news this graciously? Right. Underlings now in charge and bossing him around? With David's industrial-sized ego? As if. This fairytale happens when? The second Tuesday of next week.

But given everything we'd gone through, who was to say? Maybe the guy was more pragmatic than I'd given him credit for. The guy had a family. The guy had expenses. The guy was no kid. The guy needed a job. And he might find the pickings in the industry right now rather slim for the captain steering the wheel of a sinking ship. So, he wasn't the head honcho. And? It suited him just fine when Butch took over. Maybe he'd be good with us running the company? A paycheck was a paycheck. Put a smile on his face, keep his big mouth shut, not be responsible for everything working like a fine-tuned instrument, not be blamed if it all went to hell in a handbasket, and still get paid a bucket of bucks each Friday.

David flashed a hundred-thousand-watt smile. "I've been negotiating with a funding company to back me financially to buy Mermaid out of bankruptcy." David's eyes shone with excitement. "We're close to an agreement. Once it's done, the offer will be submitted to the court for acceptance. I am almost positive the offer will be accepted. Fingers crossed; we should be good to go in time for the Miami Swimwear Market."

I choked on my wine. Holy guacamole. Was it possible to get it any more wrong?

David went on. "Even though it isn't soup yet, it will be. Please understand I'm working night and day to ensure Mermaid's future and yours."

One of us needed to stop David before he made a complete fool of himself. Queenie and Gary suddenly developed paralysis of the mouth. So, I interrupted David. I tried speaking cryptically to ease him into it. "David, I'm afraid you're a day late and a dollar short."

David Workman was a man used to being in charge. David Workman was not a man you interrupt. The purple vein in the middle of his forehead pulsed with fury. He spat venom. "What are you talking about?" Anger at my disrespect flamed red from his neck to his hairline. Yet fear clouded his eyes. David nervously looked around the table. "Are all of you leaving and not told me yet?" Pleading softened his tone. "Please don't. I am serious. We're just about done." He crossed his heart. "I swear, if you'll only bear with me a little longer, it will be finalized soon."

I smiled sardonically. "Nope. Not it at all."

David spoke through clenched teeth. "Then. What. Is. It?"

"David," Queenie miraculously rediscovered her vocal cords. "A formal announcement will be made at the end of next week. Holly, Gary, and I teamed up with a financial group, and *we've bought Mermaid*." Queenie stood between Gary and me and put an arm around our shoulders. "The court *accepted our offer* and all the papers are signed. It's a *done deal. We're* the *new owners* of Mermaid Swimwear."

David turned white as chalk as he clutched the back of his chair. His jaw bunched, but his words remained clogged in his throat. Ike's bushy eyebrows shot to his hairline. Good grief. Was he waiting for the punchline to a joke? Bernice looked over her glasses to see if we were pulling her leg. These people were the backbone of the company. They were the ones we counted on if we were to succeed. If they weren't on board, where did it leave us? Where did it leave Mermaid?

At least no one ran out the door as if their hair was on fire…yet. So, before there was a mass exodus, I flashed my best let's-close-the-deal smile. "Will you please do us the honor of joining us in this adventure? Together we will bring Mermaid back and make her greater than ever."

My voice caught as I looked expectantly into their eyes. "We can't do it without you." I locked eyes with David. "So, are you guys with us?"

A word about the author…

Born in the Big Apple, award-winning cozy mystery author Susie Black now calls sunny Southern California home. Like the protagonist in her Holly Swimsuit Mystery Series, Susie is a successful apparel sales executive. Susie began telling stories as soon as she learned to talk. Now she's telling all the stories from her garment industry experiences in humorous mysteries.

She reads, writes, and speaks Spanish, albeit with an accent that sounds like Mildred from Michigan went on a Mexican vacation and is trying to fit in with the locals. Since life without pizza and ice cream as her core food groups wouldn't be worth living, she's a dedicated walker to keep her girlish figure. A voracious reader, she's also an avid stamp collector. Susie lives with a highly intelligent man and has one incredibly brainy but smart-aleck adult son who inexplicably blames his sarcasm on an inherited genetic defect.

Looking for more? Visit her website: www.authorsusieblack.com Sign up for her reader list and receive a free swimwear fit guide.

Or reach her at mysteries_@authorsusieblack.com